NOBODY WILL EVER LOVE YOU

NOBODY WILL EVER LOVE YOU

A.M. Howcroft

InkTears
The Granary,
Purston,
Brackley,
Northants,
NN13 5PL

Typeset by Troubador Publishing Ltd

ISBN 978-1-910207-19-2

Dedicated to those who never got the chance to read this book

CONTENTS

THE COBBLESTONES SPARKLE

Wednesday, nearly midnight.

The ground is thirty or forty metres below me. Maybe it's sixty metres, I'm not very good at judging heights. In fact, I'm not very good at judging lots of things. Like how much alcohol I can drink and not do something stupid. I'm balanced on the edge of a very slippery roof. The temperature is below freezing, and I'm only wearing a T-shirt and jeans. My shirt and jacket are knotted together as a rope, and Jani is swinging this towards me. The jacket's a fake Hugo Boss I bought at the market. I don't think the stitches are very strong. I grab the end of it and the makeshift rope is stretched between us.

Jani shouts, "I can hold you."

Jani hates me. He wants me dead. He has already punched me twice tonight, and led me into this terrifying spot. It's his idea that I swing over the huge drop to a ledge only a few centimetres wide. There is a tree underneath but if I miss that it's all cobblestones. Jani might let go of the jacket-rope, even if it doesn't break. Nobody is watching us and nobody would know. I couldn't blame him. He's my best friend.

Four hours earlier.

I get a call from Jani. He's bored and wants to hit the town. I tell him I'm strapped for cash and he says he'll lend me some until Friday.

1

"It's too cold," I say, and he sulks. "Besides," I add, "I'm tired."

"From killing chickens all day?"

That's what I do for a job. It's not actually me that kills them. I collect the scraps and incinerate those bits that even the dogs won't eat. You get used to the smell. I've got an early start tomorrow, first shift. I don't want to go out. He says that Elena might join us with some of her friends.

An hour later we're walking into town. We walk fast because it's cold. It will freeze tonight, for sure. We go to a bar hidden in a corner of the medieval city walls. It's a beautiful place, really secluded and only the locals know it so you don't have to wade through tourists to get a drink. Not that there are many tourists at this time of year. The building itself is really old and the timbers are black. People must have been much smaller in the past because I'm always hitting my head on the low beams. Tonight, I walk in very carefully and stay stooped. They have a special hot toddy, which is strong as an onion, and Jani orders two.

"Let's sit outside," he says. He's always been a bit crazy.

In summer, the gardens are amazing. Crammed full of laughter and conversation, a young crowd with a buzz. There are three gardens squashed around different sides of the building. Tonight, it's absolutely deserted apart from us and an acoustic guitarist. He's employed for the price of free drinks to entice trade on a week night. All three of us huddle around a brazier that could do with a few more coals. The guitar man plays a slow version of *Riders on the Storm*.

"This is going to be a good year," Jani says.

"It's nearly over."

"Not for me. I always rate years from September to September."

"We're not at school anymore."

"It's not that. Fall is when the year really turns, isn't it?"

"When everything dies."

"Nothing dies. The trees shed the old stuff, the rubbish. They think. Then they begin growing. You can't see it until the spring, but it's happening."

Jani is a dreamer. He always seems to have different ideas to the rest of us. Most of the time they come to nothing, but I enjoy hearing them. He is a touch under two metres tall, same as me, but slightly more solid. He has a round face like a hamster, which is covered in stubble because he hates shaving. That's what he says, anyway. I think he wants to look like Brad Pitt. I borrow some cash from him and get the next drinks so I can warm up inside the bar. I smack my head on one of the low beams and spill most of my toddy on the way out. Elena has arrived, on her own.

"Hey." We air kiss on both cheeks.

She sits on Jani's lap. She's not that light and Jani shifts his legs to distribute her weight. Elena is always so cheerful. I think she has the prettiest face of any of Jani's girlfriends and a lovely smile, Hollywood teeth.

"How's the writing?" she asks me.

"What writing?" says Jani.

"The poetry. You are looking at the next Hora." She gives me one of her special smiles.

"Well, I've not done as much as I'd like lately, you know… work…"

"You should. You *must*." She turns to Jani, "He's good."

"I've never heard any. When did you hear his poetry?"

Half of me is feeling awkward. The other half feels good.

She closes her eyes. "Entwined in silk, your hand might wave languorously, above the drenched walls of Troy…"

"When did you do that?" Jani is looking to me for the answer.

"I'm not sure, maybe the party at your apartment."

"No," she says, eyes still closed. "Don't you remember?"

I put my drink down and rub my hands to keep them warm.

3

The glass is empty. Jani shifts Elena off his lap and slides towards me along the bench.

"Don't you remember?" he mimics her.

"I remember," I say.

"I bet you do!"

He punches me in the shoulder, playfully. Or at least, I think it was playfully. It makes my arm go numb, but I laugh as though it's all a big joke.

"You're jealous," she says to Jani, as though shocked, then repeats it with a knowing tone. She squeezes his hamster cheeks and bends over to kiss him. I get a view of her arse. Those jeans are tight.

Elena can't stay. "Early start for work," she explains. She blows me a kiss as she vanishes around the corner.

"My bladder has shrunk to the size of a pea," I say and wander off to relieve the tension.

When I get back, Jani has gone. I assume he has left to follow Elena. The guitar man nods his head towards the other garden, and continues his version of some Stones classic. I find Jani tucked in the corner, with the city walls towering behind him.

"Ko-ko-ko," he says. That's one of his favourite jokes. "Over here chicken-boy. I could smell you anywhere." You would have said cluck. And cock-a-poodle-poo. I can talk about chickens in any language.

I think about calling it a night, but I see he has collected two beers. He hands me one.

"So, you and Elena?" he smiles ironically.

"What do you mean?"

He takes a slug of beer and wipes the moustache off before answering.

"Do you trust me?" he asks.

"With what?"

4

"Either you trust someone or you don't."

"It depends. Everything is about the situation." He doesn't look convinced, so I go on, "I trust my doctor. I'd let him prescribe some drugs to get rid of a cough, but I wouldn't let him perform brain surgery on me."

"You're getting trust and responsibility mixed up. Being held accountable for your job is one thing. If you don't clean up the chicken shit you get fired."

"That last bit's true."

"You see, trust is blind faith. It's letting me do your brain surgery."

"No, that's madness. I wouldn't let you near me with a scalpel."

"Trust is madness. It's about being irrational. People aren't machines who only do things out of self-interest."

"Aren't they?"

"Do you think people would do whatever they wanted if they thought they could get away with it?"

"Probably."

"We're better than that."

Jani stands up and necks his drink.

"I'll show you," he says.

He turns his back and places one foot carefully on the wall that runs parallel to the building. His other foot he places on the opposing wall, so he straddles both and is nestled deep in the right-angled corner. The stones are large but rough and he grabs two hand-holds at head height.

Then he says, "Follow me."

Next thing, he begins springing up the wall. Not really climbing, he uses his legs in a rigid way, locking them out and then pushing up in a mini-jump. He scales the wall at a frightening pace. I shout and he yells in exhilaration. I have to take a few paces back to watch properly. His right foot is on the old city structure, but the left wall is formed by stones from the high bell tower of a church. Like a spider pulling himself up a thread he makes jerky movements and then soars, as though he's attached to the bell tower. My breath comes out in silver clouds as I tilt my head back. At the top of the city wall, which is still some fifteen or twenty metres below the peak of the bell tower, he clambers on to the walkway and turns to wave.

"Come on up," he shouts. "You've always wanted to."

I have never had any desire to climb the walls, although Jani has often talked about it on drunken summer evenings.

"The view's magnificent."

"I'm staying down here."

"Oh no you're not," he says and dangles something in the air. It's small and black but I can't work out what it is at first, then I have a sinking feeling. My wallet.

"Bastard!"

I plant a foot on each wall and try to copy his technique for bouncing up. It's much easier than I thought. In fact, it's so easy that I quite enjoy it. When I get about three quarters of the way up I suddenly realise how high I've come, and how easily I could plummet. My legs begin to shake and my tongue sticks to my mouth as though I've been drinking glue. I stop.

"Keep moving," Jani says.

I struggle for the last few feet and he yanks my hand and pulls me on to the ledge. We look over the battlements, those see-saw bits. I forget the word. The city is laid out for us, sparkling in the perfect cold air. Jani says it looks like a treasure chest that's been kicked over, spilling jewels across the ground. I think it looks like one of those photos of another galaxy where each tiny dot is another sun and you feel really small and insignificant.

I turn to say something and find Jani walking along the ledge, heading into the old town, passing the tower and wandering the walls' zigzag route that reveals the original boundary. I shuffle behind him, keeping a tight hold of the wall. He stops on top of a small supporting buttress, with a square area of a few feet where we can both stand. Unlike the tourist sections of the wall, this has no handrails.

"Hit me," he says and pats his stomach.

"Haven't we done enough tonight?"

"Go on," he says. "Hard. I'm ready." He braces.

You never want to hit too hard. There was Houdini's death for one thing, plus the fact that your opponent gets to hit you back. That's our rule. Going first is worst, calculating how hard to hit. I feel strangely liberated though. He's near the edge, but if he falls off it will be his own fault.

I swing hard. He swivels, which isn't allowed. You have to stand still and take it. I miss and stagger forward. I nearly choke on my heart, it leaps so high. I'm going to fall off. Jani grabs me before I topple. He laughs. I swear, in shock first, then anger.

"Hit me," he says again. "Give it all you've got."

This time the wall is behind him, and I don't wait for a second request. I catch him hard. He sinks back against the stones and doubles up.

"Are you OK?" I ask. He shakes his head and lets out a partial laugh.

"Good one," he coughs then asks, "my turn?"

I can't say no. We switch positions. I wait with the wall behind me. He hits hard, but with less venom than I did. I double over to mirror his actions, so he thinks the punches are equal. Otherwise he'll try harder next time.

When I've regained control I remember why I climbed the walls.

"My wallet," I say.

"Here it is."

He holds it in front of me and then when I reach for it he pulls his hand back. I lunge forward, the effect of which is simply to knock the wallet out of his hand. There's a flat roof not so far away, at about the same height as us. The wallet lands there and slides. I think for a moment it might go right over the other side but it stops not far beyond the middle.

"We can get that," says Jani. There's some restoration work taking place on the next section of wall, and Jani goes to collect a plank and pushes it out to form a bridge to the roof.

"I'll hold this end," he says.

"I'm not walking over there. You're the one that caused all this. You can go."

"It's not my wallet."

"Shit."

It's a long drop, but there's a tree beneath. I tell myself any fall will be broken, and the worst I'll get are some scratches.

"Put all your weight on it," I say.

He kneels down on one end of the plank and ducks his head since I have to step over him to get on. I keep hold of the wall to steady myself at first, then turn around and spread my arms out like a tightrope walker.

"Don't look down," Jani says.

"How am I meant to see the plank?"

I start slowly and get faster. The plank is bouncy and it gets worse the further along I go, so I walk quicker and quicker, jumping the last section to land on the roof. Thank God it doesn't give way. Jani cheers, and cautiously I move out to the centre, prodding the roof with the tip of my sneakers, hoping it's solid. I pick up the wallet and then hear Jani swear. A second or two later there's a crash far below.

Jani is still on the wall, looking at me.

"The plank fell off," he says.

"Get another."

"It was the only one."

I walk towards the edge and we stare at each other.

"It's not that far," he says.

"Oh no."

"If you ran from the other side of the roof, you could easily make it."

"No way."

"You were good at the long jump. Didn't you break a record in year eight?"

"I'm not doing it."

There's silence. We stand only a few feet apart, but are separated by a dark space that could suck either of us into it like a black hole.

"What's in the wallet?" he asks.

"Hey?"

"You said you were out of cash, so what's in the wallet that's so valuable?"

"The usual. Credit cards and stuff."

"You haven't got a credit card."

The alcohol is wearing off, and I begin to remember how cold it is. How cold I am. My fingers are going numb, my legs stiffening up.

"Take off your shirt and jacket," Jani says.

"What?"

"We can make a rope."

"No way."

"Ko-ko-ko!" he flaps some imaginary wings.

The rope doesn't sound such a bad idea, and I don't have any others. I make the best knots I know how and pull them incredibly hard to make sure they are tight. Then I throw the whole thing to Jani, since it's not quite long enough to reach, and he ties his jacket on to make it longer. Then he swings it out to me a few times until I grasp hold of it. I'm standing right on the edge, which is icy, and very slippery. The cobblestones sparkle like stars, or perhaps diamonds.

"I can hold you," Jani shouts.

"About Elena…"

"Jump."

Given everything that has happened recently, or even just tonight, I shouldn't rely on Jani. He's angry. He's drunk. He knows more than he says. Yet, as he said earlier, trust is irrational. Life would be hell without some people you can always count on. I jump.

Swinging like Tarzan, I hit the wall hard. I don't let go, and the stitches don't break, immediately. I dangle. Looking up, I see Jani straining to hold me. I can hear tiny ripping noises.

"Use your legs," he says, "push."

I scramble and push. He pulls but mostly he holds on, keeping his weight anchored and low so we don't topple to the cobblestones together. I get one hand over the edge and then another. He loops the rope over part of the wall's battlements and grabs my hands to help me roll on to the walkway. Relief floods through me. We sit back to back and listen to our breathing. I'm not so cold anymore.

"Your face is a mess," Jani says even though he is not facing me. I touch it and realise I'm bleeding. I'm not sure if I've broken my nose or split my lip. Everything is beginning to hurt. We make our way along the wall. A quarter of a mile further there are some steps where the tourist section starts, and we walk down to street level. He wants me to go to the hospital. I go home instead.

In my room, I wash my face and check for damage. My lip is swollen but nothing seems to be broken. I take my wallet, open it and remove my picture of Elena. I screw it up and drop it in the bin.

BREEDING MONSTERS

My mobile rings to the tune of *The Lion Sleeps Tonight*. Janet gives me a look, that says, "if this call is work you're dead".

I flick open the clamshell. It's work. I study Janet while I listen to the caller. Janet looks beautiful. Her dress dazzles, with black silk and sequins clustered like stars. I listen to the appalling news. Just when I think my life is coming together, it falls apart. The call ends.

"Felicity?" Janet asks. Clearly, she was studying me too.

I nod. "It's bad. I should look in, briefly."

"They know it's our anniversary," she says.

"Let me call you a cab and meet you at the restaurant. I'll be quick."

Janet chews her lip, messing the perfect line of red lipstick. She knows how much it means. Ten years dedicated to one goal and I've failed again. My professional credibility is at stake and more importantly our funding grant.

"If it isn't meant to be…" she squeezes my arm.

My Land Rover is painfully slow, but once rolling it's harder to stop than a rhino. Charging past the wooden tiger at the Park entrance I hit the button to lower my window and then stamp on the brakes, skidding to a halt at the security lodge. I feel a fool in my dinner jacket but hardly anyone will be here. I realise I'm wearing aftershave, which is banned. You don't want to smell like a sow in heat when stepping in to an enclosure with a sexually-starved tiger. There's no time to shower, though.

"Doctor." The guard acknowledges me and lifts the barrier.

I speed through the Park and finally leave the car skewed across two spaces. There's rain falling but it's only a short run to the centre. Swiping my card, I enter and stride past three white tigers. Sheets of industrial strength glass separate us and hopefully shield my aftershave.

"Hi," Michelle passes me an overall. "I wasn't sure whether to call, being that it's your anniversary." Her nostrils twitch suspiciously.

"You did the right thing. How's Felicity?"

"Physically, she seems fine. Licked herself for a while but she's settled again. We've kept her isolated. I wasn't sure if you'd want to inspect her."

We peer through the observation chamber's one-way glass.

"Miscarriages are a fact of nature," I say, glad my wife can't hear me.

Felicity lifts her pale head. She sniffs ostentatiously although she can't possibly trace us in here. She's nine foot from nose to tail. In between lies 125kg of bone and muscle and two blue eyes bright enough to set the proverbial forests alight. She's my eldest. I raised her from a cub. Every tiger has a unique pattern of stripes, distinctive as a fingerprint or a snowflake. Felicity has two bold stripes curling around her white forearms like smoke, contrasted by dark flame-patterns encircling her face.

Our tigers have contraceptive implants placed beneath the skin when they're chipped so that they can't reproduce. There's no shortage of tigers in zoos. We could easily breed but every legitimate zoo is already over quota. I sometimes fantasize about releasing them into the wilds of Solihull. They would adapt well. The nimbys would moan about the occasional teenager eaten on a street corner, but that would be a positive advantage from my perspective.

We do have authority to breed from Felicity. My special project. All white tigers are Bengals with two recessive genes. Genetic science is helping us move towards the last great threshold; the black tiger. This would be a true melanistic, without stripes – not the pseudo-variety.

"What have we got?" I say. "Blood? Any evacuation?"

Michelle shows me the tissue mass.

"Felicity ate the rest," she states.

"That's normal," I say. Michelle's a good assistant but I keep her at arms length. In my profession, never get too close is not a cliché but practical guidance. I sometimes wonder about Michelle.

I consider sedating Felicity to perform a scan. That would kiss goodbye to dessert with Janet and see me sleeping in the spare room for a week. Besides, this is finished. All we can do is keep Felicity under observation, skip a cycle and wait for her to enter estrus again.

"Let her rest while I review these," I say.

Michelle sets up the equipment and retreats. I peer at the display, looking for anything to identify. We've had very few miscarriages. I was certain we had the genetic puzzle solved. This was going to be the first melanistic in captivity. The only verifiable black tiger in the world although they do occur naturally. James Forbes' lost watercolour is a mild proof, surviving in written descriptions of the black and glossed purple coat apparently variegated like rich velvet. Then there were the three cubs at Oklahoma City Zoo in the 70s, where the mother mysteriously killed the two darkest animals herself. With a world population of a few thousand tigers, I seriously doubt whether there's one alive today. Declining tiger populations suggest we may never see another. If we do it will almost certainly be a dead specimen, the myths will ensure the veracity of that.

You see, the rural regions maintain their legends. If the white tiger is a ghost then the black is a demon. They pad through the night devouring souls, stealing dreams, causing drought and disease, even withering crops as they swagger past. The value of a demon's corpse to the Chinese apothecaries would be immeasurable. No black tiger would survive in the wild. If we can produce one in the West Midlands, we'll have achieved something remarkable. This is the beneficial application of genetics, ignored by the media. Not breeding monsters, but conserving and educating, revealing that animals are beautiful and fearsome in equal measure. Just like us.

"Let's hope San Diego fares better," Michelle murmurs.

"Everyone wants that first black cub," I say.

"Nero would've been a good name."

"Burning brightly, eh?" I smile. "The Marketeers will hijack the naming process."

"Can I do anything?" she asks.

"No, thanks. I'll take a quick look, must dash…"

"The restaurant," she says.

"Exactly."

She returns to the observation chamber.

I hate San Diego. Copy cats. Stealing my research, pumping huge funds from Hollywood celebrities into their projects. In my more paranoid phases I wonder if they have a spy in our labs.

"That can't be," I say aloud.

I zoom.

"No."

If "eureka" is a moment of brilliant inspiration then there ought to be a word for the slower revelation. One that waxes at the moon's pace, an immense knowledge pulling everything towards it with irresistible gravity. This word could describe the situation where you already know the answer but can't admit the truth until the whole image is laid bare.

I drag myself to the next machine. Placing a sample in the tube, I bang it on and watch it spin out of my control. Science is no longer run on Newton's fixed laws; more Heisenberg, uncertainty and chaos. The new century erodes and blurs our stringent ethical guidelines that have governed since Victorian times. Things are harder to compartmentalise. We're not different people at home and work; the edges are complicated to define. I'm not a scientist and a husband I'm the compound result. It's beginning to look like that equals a complete failure.

The analysis terrifies me. It reveals that the tiger's miscarried cub was human. My brain grinds through that logic. Felicity was impregnated with a human foetus. A truth leading to several inexorable conclusions. I check the results but that's a forlorn exercise. Resting my head in my hands, I fight to control my breathing. Michelle mustn't hear. I seal the remaining materials in a container. I want to hurl it across the room and smash the equipment. Instead, I push the container into a jiffy envelope and tuck it under my arm. I almost forget to clear the images off the computer. This may end my career as well as my marriage.

I try to leave without encountering Michelle but she's silent as a cat. We all pick up something of the animals we study.

"Are you alright?" she asks.

"Bitterly disappointed."

"You've got a lot invested in this project."

"More than you can imagine," I say and regret my words immediately.

I head for the exit. "Call me if you need to."

She watches me run across the gravel and I can feel her eyes burning into my back. It's raining harder. Janet will be waiting in the restaurant, letting her anger build. I release mine as I hit the main road, overtaking on blind corners, flashing my lights, roaring abuse as I hurtle past cars. In town, my anger fizzles and sparks as I slow down and try to compose myself.

Janet is surprisingly relaxed, tapping her feet to the live pianist and finishing a cocktail. I look dishevelled. My coat is with the maître d', but water drips from my hair and nose. I kiss Janet and sit down. The waiter offers a menu and asks what I want to drink.

"Are we having red?" I ask Janet.

"Not for me," she smiles.

"Of course," I say, looking at her cocktail.

"Virgin daiquiri," she answers my glance.

I order a large Cab Sauvignon. I need something rich and heavy, thick as blood. Something to numb the pain.

"It's funny," Janet says. "I'm calm. It feels different this time."

"That's good." I can't decide if it is.

"How's Felicity?" she asks.

The waiter interrupts. I've not looked at the menu but Janet speaks.

"I'm famished. Do you mind if I order while you choose?"

"Go ahead," I say.

"I'll have the caesar salad to start, no dressing and can you make sure it's all freshly washed?" The waiter looks puzzled and she indicates her tummy with a semi-circle motion.

"Madame," he replies.

"Then I'll take the fillet. Medium rare."

I look up, startled at her choice.

"I mean well-done. Nearly forgot. I'm craving it raw. One of those things."

There's no ethical dilemma. I have to tell her. My wife is pregnant and unless I'm very much mistaken, she's carrying a black tiger. There's no chance of the pregnancy lasting. It's only a matter of time before she too aborts. All I can do is speed the process and ease the physical pain. Even if it were technically possible for her to carry the tiger until it was feasible, it would be immensely cruel to let it progress.

Here I sit, one of the world's leading experts on animal fertility and I can't produce a baby of my own. I know people laugh about

16

me. There's nothing wrong with my sperm or Janet's eggs. We're victims of that rising human epidemic known as unexplained infertility. We should have tried starting a family when we were younger, but we didn't meet until we were both in our mid-thirties. It feels like fate is toying with us like a cat with a mouse.

I can't remember whose idea it was first. We both knew the risks. We wanted something to share as we grew older instead of stale conversations and silent blame. *Can we give nature a helping hand?* I do remember Janet saying that. The clinics weren't interested, given our age and the length of the waiting lists. Yet, it was a simple procedure with my background and I had all the equipment. Do-It-Yourself IVF. I labelled everything so carefully; I don't understand how it happened. I need more time and wine before I tell her. Tonight, we need to enjoy our anniversary and celebrate hope.

During the meal, I can't help but imagine a tiger curled inside her. Kicking, stretching, scraping, a miniature black demon with talons instead of claws.

San Diego will take the glory. This delay means success will fall into their hands. I may get a citation if they're generous but I won't get any more research dollars. Yet, the world's only black tiger is alive right now, feeding off expensive steak that I'm paying for, smouldering with burgeoning intelligence. If only there was some way to transfer it from Janet to one of the tigers.

"Have you thought about names?" Janet asks.

"I'm a little superstitious," I say, although I think *Nero*. "I want to make sure everything is OK first."

"The scan's next Thursday," she says. "I can't stop thinking about it."

"Me neither." That's my deadline. We have to resolve this before then.

I know I should tell her now, but the scene would be horrendous. She would scream and knock the table over. She

17

might try to rip her own womb out or stab the tiger with a steak knife. Alternatively, her anger may be directed at me or she could faint. There are so many factors to consider. I watch her devour pudding while I sip a black coffee. We drive home and I almost tell her in the car. I nearly say something when we undress for bed. I come close to confessing before we turn the light off.

My dreams are ravaged by blazing fires. Rome burns and velvet-skinned tigers pace the forests surrounding the city. I'm woken by a scream. Janet's not in bed. I leap up. Over the banister I see the orange lamp switched on between the lounge and kitchen. I rush downstairs and hear her sobs. Janet is curled in a foetal position, night-clothes soaked in sweat and blood. She leans her head against the leather armchair.

"Pain," is the one word she manages to say.

My eyes scan the chair. In a spasm her fingernails have gouged tracks down the seat like claw marks. The miscarriage has started. She stiffens as another wave of agony sweeps over her.

"Let's go," I say.

I collect my car keys and throw on some clothes. I can't quite shake my mental image of a small black demon snarling in her womb. As I dash down the stairs it occurs to me that the Safari Park is a fraction closer than the Hospital. It has a full range of medical equipment and no prying eyes, except for Michelle. I'm sure I could deal with that small problem. What is it they say, risk and opportunity always go hand-in-hand? Accidents do happen.

At the top of the road I can turn left to the Hospital or right to the Safari Park.

I hesitate. A catastrophe is not one bad decision, but a cascade of tiny choices. I can see that. Once you've started down a path each choice is easier, more natural then the last. Even the hardest decisions are out of our hands, in many ways. Janet lies in the back, unaware of the choices that lie before us.

The legend says the black tiger is a monster, a devil made flesh.

As I said before, we all take on some aspects of the creatures we study.

I turn right.

DRIFTWOOD

The cove had a reputation for danger that it worked hard to maintain. Each year it swallowed at least one victim to spit out further down the coast. Perhaps it was the risks that made her return so often. She had always been attracted to things that refused to be tamed. The waves were certainly wild today. Even this high up she could hear the pebbles rattling as the sea dragged them away. She passed Ned and his wire-haired terrier in the car park. They nodded to each other and muttered something incomprehensible that passed for a welcome. Ned drove away as she headed along the narrow path to the cliff. The wind had an edge that could slice and toss you into the sea like a discarded fish head. She steadied herself on the rail. These were the best days for her work. Although the tide had slipped its treasures ashore many hours ago, nobody would have disturbed them.

Silhouetted by the falling sun she moved below the line of rock marking the top of the cliff. The lichen was stained red by the evening rays and bronzed ferns added a rusty glow to the far reaches of the cove. Plunging recklessly down the path she was unaware of the eyes tracking her progress. With a satisfying crunch she jumped onto the grey stones that dominated the beach. Pausing for a moment, she scanned the horizon, her dark eyes clouded. Spotting her first quarry, she moved across the bay, oblivious to the hidden observer.

★

Years ago, the shop had meant everything to her. Now, it was either too quiet and she worried about the money, or else too busy. She loathed the people that squeezed into her tiny shop like whitebait, whipping around in a ball with their rucksack tails knocking things over. There was still pleasure in coaxing shapes from the wood, though, finding the secret submerged within. Some were strong designs that cried out from the first moment she saw them snared by the tide. Others were subtler and she had to feel the texture and caress the surfaces before an image would suggest itself. There were many pieces without a soul and she felt no pity in turning them into dolphins or mermaids to abate the frenzy of feeding tourists. Stopping abruptly, she tilted her head to one side as though she'd caught a trace of derision on the wind.

You can laugh if you like, she thought, *but you were the one who condemned me to slavery for tourists. In the sixteen years since you uprooted me, I've only found a handful of real pieces, rich woods with the capacity for art. The beauty might be in the grain or a pattern of knots around which the sculpture has to dance. These pieces need time to reveal their true nature. Sometimes they lie in the studio for weeks before whispering their desires. You were a lot faster to state your demands. Only one piece spoke to me immediately, the oak pleading to be Thomas Cranmer. You said I must have read too many historical novels. I was able to represent him at that crucial moment, with eyes turned to heaven as smoke curled around the stake and the first flames beckoned. Nobody ever bought him and he holds sway in a corner of the shop, significantly overpriced to ensure he remains there. You could never see the point, though. "What use is a martyr in a souvenir shop?" That was your line. We have two, I should have said.*

She swept a few mediocre items of driftwood into her fraying string bag. Not satisfied with rattling stones, the sea reached for larger rocks and hurled waves at the headland to cast a white spray in the air like a fisherman's net. She stopped to watch a lone crab running from one pool to another.

Sometimes, I think of you that way, she thought. *Inside your armoured shell, scurrying from place to place while looking for a shiny pebble that turns out to be glass from a broken bottle. Did you find what you wanted? Whatever it was you left me for. You never had the courage to risk anything that mattered.*

She scooped an apple-shaped stone from the shoreline and tossed it back to the writhing waves. A figure emerged from the rocks to one side, slightly behind her. She sensed his presence and whipped around aggressively.

"What are you doing here?"

He continued his approach and took several paces before quietly replying.

"Is that any way to greet a friend?"

She bit her lip and for a moment exposed the vulnerable woman of sixteen years ago. The look faded and any thought of apology drained away. Her voice was colder than the sea.

"It's late."

"I was passing by," he said. "Have you found your next Cranmer?"

"I thought you hated him."

"No, he was magnificent. Art with a capital A. I just thought the face looked too familiar."

She spluttered, "You still don't think it was meant to be you?"

"All the customers would point at me and laugh."

"You gave them good reason."

He stared into her bitter eyes and avoided any riposte. She waited for him to reveal the reason for this mysterious return. He only wished there was an answer that could satisfy her. In his mind there were only questions, and perhaps that was all there had ever been between them.

"I found something for you." He turned and walked across the cove without looking back to see if she would follow. She kept pace and was alongside him when he halted and nodded towards the rocks.

"Oh my God," she said.

Held captive, between a pair of boulders, was half a tree. It was all in one beautiful, battered carcass. Her experienced eye could tell immediately it was not a native. This reeked of the exotic, of spice and profound heat. She clambered on to the rocks and brushed her fingers along the surface to soak up the textures. The salt-ridden bark was coarse but the exposed portions of trunk gave a sensation of polished ebony, transformed to amber by the sun.

"Rio. It has to be Rio."

He shrugged, "I thought it looked good."

"Give me a hand."

He was relieved that the awkwardness of the encounter was temporarily forgotten. With him at the roots and her holding the splintered section they tried to heave it over the rocks. The weight was immense, but then he already knew that. Without Ned's help he would never have been able to hurl the trunk far enough off the cliffs to avoid it shattering on the rocks. Ned was a good man. Strong, despite his age and taciturn to the extreme. The two of them had struggled with the tree that had been wedged into his Land Rover for a week. It would have been easier to give her the wood but she would never accept it as a gift, especially from him. Her best work had always come after an argument, passion following fury. An impulse had made him return to fire her muse.

"Perhaps we should try to snap the end off?" he suggested.

"No. That's the head."

"The head?"

"This is Lilith. You can see the body here," she pointed to the midsection, "with her torso twisted away, shielding herself against them."

"Them?" he asked.

"Adam and God, battling to control her fecundity."

"We haven't got time for a feminist rant. We need to move it fast."

The light was failing and they were both aware of the new tide coiling around them.

"You're just like them aren't you?" this was an accusation.

"Who?"

"When I couldn't provide you with a son, you left. That was it."

"Don't talk rubbish."

There wasn't much conviction in his voice. They stood looking at each other over the darkening body of the tree. The white foam gleamed as it slithered along the edge of the cove.

He broke the silence, "Let's go."

"You're going to walk away again."

"The tide's coming in," he said.

"I'm not leaving yet."

"It's just a log."

"It's Lilith," she replied. "And I don't walk away from the things I love."

"We'll drown together if we stay," he commented.

"So that was it?"

He paused, caught in another one of her conversational traps. It had been a mistake to return.

"We always were better apart," he responded.

"Help me."

"It's too late for that." He turned and missed her faint answer.

Stumbling, he made his way towards the path, feet crunching down hard as though he were grinding bones. She watched his figure fade into darkness. Then she looked at the tree. She'd often wondered what it would be like to be driftwood, floating from one destination to the next with no commitments. A life of freedom and casual pleasures, unencumbered by duty or purpose. A life bereft of meaning.

Pulling a silver wire with a thick plastic coating from her pocket she wound the cord three times around the trunk and hooked a loop over a narrow section of the taller rock. Tying a knot she sealed the open ends of the line with a padlock. The trunk would float with the tide but the rock would keep it anchored.

"That should keep you safe Lilith. I'll see you tomorrow."

Patting the wood she confidently made her way back to the path. The wind had lost its bite and even the lashing water seemed powerless. She sensed that Lilith would be her masterpiece.

Beetles & Butterflies

I shove both hands into my jeans pockets to stop myself turning blue. This thin shirt is designed for an over-heated bar, not for freezing my balls off in a deserted village. Finally, Simon finishes performing open-heart surgery on his Beetle. It's a grey-import with left-hand drive and makes a chugging noise more like a train than a car. Simon has wild black hair. Too much if you ask me, but he gets plenty of attention. His philosophy is that we should act on impulse, which works OK if you've got the looks. He's a rally driver, or will be soon. At the moment he earns his money as a courier, shifting brown packages from one business to another, while we are meant to be in lessons. Not that anyone at school notices, the teachers are too busy screwing each other, one way or another.

We accelerate into the night and he slams on the anchors at the junction, then wheel spins for effect as we turn down the lane. The heater is blasting, but it's still colder than the Lido in February. That's because the sun roof is open. Simon has a solid wood cue, one-piece. Any other car would be fine, but with the Beetle's curves the cue won't fit unless we poke it through the sunroof.

"I heard Gilksey's going to get married," he shakes his head.

"Not to that girl at the Foxes?"

"She's pregnant."

"Shit."

"Promise me something," he says. I look at him, but he keeps his eyes on the road. "You won't let me get married before I'm thirty."

"Why not?"

"I want to live a real life. I need to jump out of planes. I want to sleep with a French girl in a field where the grass sways. Or capture the first yeti and release it back into the wild without telling anyone. I don't want to be stuck at home changing nappies at twenty. All that shit."

"You don't need to be married to get caught. Which French girl?"

"Promise me." He was serious.

"What if you change your mind? Twelve years is nearly an eternity."

"I'm bound to change my mind. That's why you have to promise."

I'm used to driving with him, but it still scares the hell out of me. I once thought this was what it meant to rally, skimming along roads so fast the oaks lean over, as you keep your eyes fixed on the vanishing point. One day he really went for it and I understood this other driving was just his normal street performance. Rally work is two notches up.

I stamp on an imaginary brake seconds before we reach the corner, while he continues to accelerate. He takes the racing line. That's the angle everyone claims to know, but at these speeds the car only sticks to the tarmac for Simon. He bullets up the skinny road at the back of Barford-St-Michael. The field on the left rises up with wrinkled furrows from the Middle Ages. We nearly take off at the crest and I thank a God I don't believe in that nobody is coming the other way. The roads are rough and pot-holed, with large chunks of tractor mud waiting to slide us into the hawthorn. Approaching the junction with the main road he switches his lights off for three seconds. There are no other beams, so he fires across the junction at about ninety. I wonder what the chances are that somebody else knows the same trick.

"I had an amazing idea last night," he said.

"What?"

"Just before I fell asleep, I thought, this is it. I've got the whole thing sorted."

"What thing?"

"Life. What to do, how to win. It was beautiful. I almost got up to write it down. It was so perfect. Everything just fell into place. Exquisite."

"So what's the answer?"

"I couldn't remember a thing this morning. A bad case of mind wipe. All that was left were some clouds of dust swirling in my head. I've still got that sweet sensation, though."

I hope we can drive to Edge Hill, where we spent last summer finding satellites hidden amongst the stars. You can smell the history there, and the world seems fixed and solid. Sometimes I wonder why he drives so fast. I asked him once, as we hammered down a Roman road pinned to the horizon. Simon said he drove that way because everything else was too safe. Looking sideways out of the window, the whole world's a blur. There are so many choices to make. Things moved more slowly when I was ten. In one day we could make forts in haystacks, catch a handful of stickleback that would be dead before we got home, and sprint through the barley with a farmer spitting threats at our backs. Six weeks of school holidays could stretch out of sight. My brother would laugh if I told him that, he's always telling me I should see how fast things happen when you're twenty-five. He still treats me like a kid.

We were through Hempton in a flash. I spotted a horse in the paddock, with a thick coat. My hands and feet were on fire from the heat blasting out of the vents, but my head was still frozen because of the open sunroof. First stop was Adderbury, where a pub had resisted the urge to become a restaurant. A pool table, permanently shrouded in smoke, lurked in the back. Simon took his cue and lined up some coins on the table, while I got the drinks. Nobody asks your age in the villages. We don't drink much anyway. We can't afford to.

It was winner stays on. Simon thrashed the old bloke hogging the table. This is our Saturday night; village to village, shoot some pool, drink a little and survive on a diet of dry-roasted peanuts. Later, we stared at some girls and played spoof to decide who should approach them first. They'd left before we finished. Not that they were that special anyway.

"So where do the good ones go?" he asks, as we cruise back home via the town.

"Maybe they don't go out at night."

"Like reverse vampires, melting in the moonlight?"

"I heard there was a place in Oxford near a teacher training college, packed full of women without a man in sight."

"Urban myth. I heard it was near the nurse's hall of residence."

"Where's that?"

"God knows."

"Yee-hah!" he yells, performing a handbrake turn at the corner. "It's snowing!"

A couple of large flakes fall into the car, and I catch one in my hand like a butterfly. Within a minute, we are in a blizzard. I can barely see a thing but Simon senses his way through the suburban streets. We drive out of town and climb towards the more isolated villages. We stop briefly at the twenty-four hour petrol station. I give him a fiver towards the fuel and he puts the same in himself, chucking two king-size Mars Bars through the sun roof as he walks back to the car.

I twist the volume up and we listen to some old tracks and gorge on chocolate. The road is getting progressively more difficult, and the rear-wheels slide as we corner. Simon controls it without any apparent concern.

"I am never going to die," I tell him.

"Me neither. Why waste all this?"

"I just know we're immortal."

"Isn't everybody?" we laugh.

By the time our Beetle reaches Hornton the world has gone white. It seems to have been snowing longer here, although it has stopped now. The inside of the car is soaked. We should have stopped to drop Simon's cue at his house, but his parents would have asked too many questions. The moon is bright, and the sky is shockingly clear. We pass a few cars on the main road, but nobody is out in the village. The hill presses its face against the snow, resembling a monster straining to break through the surface. Simon pauses at the crest and gazes at the valley beyond. We didn't talk much on the way here. I was too busy dreaming. At night, my thoughts are optimistic. They leap ploughed fields and soar past hedgerows, travelling away from this town to a new life in London.

"We're here," he says.

I hadn't realised there was a planned destination. It is quite normal to race randomly through this rural labyrinth, Simon testing his skills and memory down lanes he can traverse in his dreams, and probably does. He smiles.

"This is it," he says, pointing ahead. "That hill. We should be able to reach the top if we pick up enough speed. The trick is to keep it on the road on the way down."

"Why here?"

"I want to see how far we can go."

It's exhilarating, sliding through the muffled silence. The speed comes on slow at first and Simon goes quiet with concentration, brushing the wheel left and right as he anticipates our snaking descent, the back flicking out whenever he applies a little too much power. We pass the dip at a good pace and he eases on more power. The angle begins to feel steep, and the speed drains off rapidly.

"Come on, baby," he yells.

We will the car forwards but it's clear we're going to stop twenty or thirty feet from the summit. I leap out and run behind to push but there's no traction.

"Climb on the back!" he shouts.

I climb up, hoping the bumper will hold. I push up and down like a kangaroo, trying to give the wheels some extra bite.

The moon's crooked smile leers at us, like a teacher that's asked you a difficult question. I climb back in, shaking from the cold. Simon explains his new plan. The hill we've come down is lower but still formidable to climb back up. We need to reverse our track. The problem is that the car is facing the wrong direction, and the drifts either side conceal ditches. This is no place for a three-point turn. Halfway down the hill there's a wider patch. He will reverse as fast as possible, handbrake turn, and try to keep our momentum so the speed can catapult us over the top of the smaller summit. We should be home by half one. I have visions of us rolling back and forward like a marble, eventually settling at the bottom of the valley.

"Ready?" he asks.

"Let's go."

We pick up speed much faster than last time and scream encouragement at the Beetle as we stare over our shoulders at the road. As the wide stretch approaches, I remember from last summer that it's a passing place before a stone bridge, when it's not draped with snowdrifts.

"Yee-hah!" he shouts for the second time, "I've got it!"

31

I grip the grab handle.

He dips the clutch and pulls the handbrake and the car obligingly flicks sideways.

"Life," he shouts again, "the beautiful life, I've remembered!"

The car flips over.

KILLER

In ten minutes, I'll be dead. Nobody will notice.

"They've found Veronica Martin's body," Steve growls.

The name is familiar, but I can't place it. I'm getting paranoid about my memory as I get older. I stare at Steve's square face, wondering if I might gather a clue about Veronica's identity. Steve looks the same as when we were at school. I don't. I'm losing hair and gaining weight in some kind of inverse proportional relationship.

"She was stuffed into a plastic box," Steve says. "They found it at the bottom of a cesspit by Nether Thorpe."

"Steve." Amy gives him a look. "We're eating."

He shrugs and forks a scallop into his mouth.

We don't see Steve and Amy very frequently. Our friendship is a little rusty, but worth lubricating with wine and good food every so often. I have eight minutes of life remaining.

"I can't believe you missed it," Amy says.

"I never bother with the news," I reply.

My wife shudders. "The news is so depressing. They only cover the recession, Middle East wars, murder and abducted children, and themselves," she collects the plates. Then I remember Veronica. Relief is my primary response. It means I haven't succumbed to Alzheimer's yet, like my mother.

Veronica Martin was at our school. She had a boyish face with a warm smile that was quirky, off-centre but full of laughter. Her hair was short, dark brown with a kiss-curl that fell over her forehead. Physically, she was small and curvy, yet still athletic and loose-limbed in her own way. I liked her. She wasn't a fashionable person to be attracted to, but she had a unique quality. Veronica disappeared when we were sixteen. The story was all over the national papers. Her parents gave the press one of those school photos that looked nothing like the girl we knew. It was splattered everywhere for weeks.

I open another bottle of wine and refill the decanter. We don't use it normally and it makes me feel like a stranger in my own home.

Veronica would be an adult now. I remember the joke.

What's the difference between Elvis and Veronica?

Most people think Elvis is still alive.

"Veronica Martin," I say. The words feel strange. "It's frightening how quickly we forget. Life steamrolls forward."

"What else can you do?" Steve replies.

I go upstairs to check on my daughter. I leave Amy and Steve debating the etiquette of raising gruesome topics during dinner. I try the stiff door into my daughter's room. The handle sticks really badly and you have to apply a lot of force. If I weren't so useless at DIY, I'd have made an attempt to fix it.

She's fast asleep with her bear cuddled tightly under one arm. She looks like an angel. My wife hates it when I say that. She doesn't like the association because angel equals dead, in her way of thinking. I close the door and return downstairs. Only a minute left before I die.

"More wine?" I say.

"Go on then." Steve holds out his glass.

"I thought you were driving?" Amy asks.

"Not now," Steve laughs.

I can see the plastic box. I can feel it, the weight and texture, the sticky edges. The plastic box in my hands, packed with colourful bits squeezing against the sides like a Chinese takeaway. I'm placing it at the bottom of the cesspit. I am the murderer. The memory is vivid and absolutely real. I can feel the damp morning air, smell the reek of the pit.

The person I was is dead. I'm not sure who I am.

Wait, this is impossible. I couldn't commit such an atrocious act and only realise it now. The human mind is powerful but this can't be true. Logically, this must be a hallucination – or a powerful empathetic response because I'm a father. There's no way a brain could eradicate a memory so completely from the conscious mind. It's been more than twenty years since she died. There would have been after-effects, some leakage. I've never had any dreams about Veronica. No recognition from reports about similar crimes. No flashbacks until now. Tell me you don't believe this could happen. Tell me.

"Hello?" Amy says. "Are you OK?"

"Sorry, miles away," I say.

"Can I get a glass of water?" she asks.

"Of course," I reply.

The water's in the utility room. I lean on the freezer and try to talk myself back into sanity. I can't have murdered someone. I would know. Anyone would. We're not robots from a sci-fi film with reprogrammable memories. Or that guy who has to write himself notes so he knows who he is when he wakes up. What the hell was that film called?

All the time, the plastic box flashes in my head like a movie scene. Each frame clicks forward in slow motion as I bend to place the box in the sewage, keeping it horizontal so nothing spills. I don't remember killing Veronica. Somebody must have cut her into pieces and crushed the dismembered parts into a see-through container. If I can't remember that, perhaps it wasn't me?

I clutch at this as evidence of my innocence. Yet, the plastic box is compelling. I have to consider there may be other memories buried so deeply I can't recall them. I fear they'll surface soon, like Veronica.

I make a detour to my office and fire up my computer. I Google memory-loss. An Amazon book is listed, *Offenders' Memories of Violent Crimes*. Amazon's Search Inside feature lets me peer within the body of text. Jargon assaults me: post traumatic stress disorder, dissociative amnesia. I read, *there are a variety of predisposing, precipitating and perpetuating biopsychosocial factors that interact to guide an offenders' memory.*

Here's my straw. I read the sentence again. It says that memory is not fixed. So it's possible my memory is false. Something I never actually did rather than an event I've forgotten. I read on and the picture turns darker. Most violent criminals fake PTSD, amnesia or both. The book lists techniques to interrogate criminals, to catch them out and prove their guilt. The introduction finishes. Amy is waiting for her drink. My wife needs help in the kitchen. The book is out of stock with a twelve-day order period. I turn to Wikipedia and search on amnesia and violent crime. All I keep hitting are references to films. I want a simple answer. Am I a murderer?

There's a second question: can a person be held responsible for a crime they didn't know they committed? I'm pretty sure I can guess the answer. Diminished responsibility is a phrase you hear on the radio when lawyers contrive to get lighter sentences for their psychopathic clients. That isn't me. I'm one of the good guys and my memory isn't diminished. It was completely missing until tonight.

My wife calls. I clear the screen and delete the history. Then I remember that Google keep the results of every search linked to IP addresses. The police probably trawl through them. I swear at my own stupidity. I need to come back later and do more searches, for their benefit and mine. Walking down the stairs I fashion other phrases I could use to show me as the victim; innocent murder, fabricated memories, paranoia, empathetic crime syndrome.

"Where have you been?" My wife whispers angrily.

"I had to check my email."

"Now?" she looks ready to kill.

I mumble a reply and wipe my face with a tea towel. I take Amy her water with a few cubes of ice. They rattle like bones as I cross the room. I ask Steve about work and try to nod and grunt in the right places to keep him talking.

Chaos whirls through my head on a wild spree, pulling open neatly filed memories, trampling and stamping them into the floor. I'll lose everything. Perhaps my parents can forgive me, but the effort will destroy them. Friends will abandon our family in droves. Emma will be bullied at school. I'll be an outcast. A target for every violent thug wanting to thrash out his anger on someone lower in the prison hierarchy. My future is a checklist of disintegration. Then again, at least I'm not a paedophile. I mean, she was only a kid, but so was I. You have to be older to be a paedophile don't you?

"How's your job going?" Amy asks, when I've left too long a gap without prompting Steve.

"Good," I say. Years of late nights hauling myself up the corporate ladder, all wasted. I imagine our beautiful home covered in graffiti and sold for peanuts to someone who doesn't care about its history as the residence of a killer. That's if they don't destroy it. I've heard the police sometimes demolish murderer's houses so nobody profits from crime. I wonder if my wife would still get an insurance pay-out. There's probably some weasel-clause that means she'll lose out.

Everything seems transparent, ghostly, although it's actually me that's fading. I can see and touch them today, but they'll be taken away. This must be a mistake. I can mentally construct a way out. Think out of the box.

I know you decided very quickly that I did it, and you're

repulsed. You tell yourself this can only happen in a story and it could never happen to you. I should send you that Amazon book. I know you won't order it for yourself. What if it says I'm right? That memory can be completely suppressed or created by circumstance and proven to be absolutely false. That would mean you too could be a murderer. You're in denial. You'll find a way to rationalize not purchasing the book; too expensive, not your sort of thing, too academic. I bet you don't even believe it exists. I dare you to check Amazon now. I can tell you feel entirely justified in not bothering. Your defence is a one hundred per cent certainty in your identity. There are no black holes in your memories, no gaps. Which is how I felt, a few minutes ago.

My wife pops her head around the door.

"Can I borrow you?" she says. "I need you to do some chopping."

My wife is so busy directing the kitchen tasks she doesn't notice anything is wrong. I feel clumsy. The knife is heavy and each slice of carrot feels like a crime as it crunches and topples on the wooden board. I catch my finger.

"It's just a nick. Better run it under the tap." She deposits a packet of Hannah Montana plasters by the sink. I hold my finger in the running water for a long time, turning it from side to side.

I'm stupid. Let's assume, hypothetically, that I'm guilty. Why would I commit such a terrible crime so badly? Why did I use a cesspit? They always get emptied. The remains were destined to surface. I left a time-bomb. Then I think of my choice of box, a see-through plastic container. How unbelievably foolish. At the very least I should have used something opaque. Even better, if I'd emptied the remains into the pit they would have decomposed. There would be nothing left after all this time. Instead, I used an airproof and water-tight box that preserved everything. Each cut available for forensic analysis. Veronica's white teeth ready to check against dental records. Her DNA and mine mixed together. I might as well have left a business card. What the hell was I thinking? I was a smart kid. Yet this was amateur, like it wasn't me at all.

I manage to hold myself vaguely together during the main course, which is a herb-crusted tenderloin. Luckily my wife likes it well done, so I don't have to see any blood swilling around on my plate. Whenever the conversation heads in the wrong direction I nudge it with a question, steering the talk towards schools, nannies and that perennial favourite, which celebrities our partners would grant us a one-night pass.

An hour ago, I considered myself a responsible parent. Now I'm manipulating conversations to cover up a murder. I wish everyone would leave me alone. I want to curl up in a corner.

"What do you think about Sophie?" Steve asks out of the blue. I begin to sweat. That case never seems to be out of the press, even after all this time. Murder sweeps back as our topic, hovering above me with pointing fingers.

"I can't tell the facts from the speculation anymore. What do you think?" my wife says.

"Well," Steve looks to Amy for approval. "We still think they did it."

"I hope so," I say too enthusiastically.

Everyone looks at me.

"If they didn't, we have to assume there are monsters waiting to kidnap our children when our backs are turned."

"That's the real world," Amy says.

"I don't believe they could hide something like that," Susan says.

"I heard they sell ten thousand more copies with her picture on the cover," Steve adds.

I shake my head, but secretly know I'm the first to stop and read the headline if I see her picture. I'm suddenly unsure if everyone does that.

"Rubber-neckers," I say. "They'd sit around the guillotine if they could."

It's all I can do to appear normal. Maintaining a conversation is an effort that nearly makes me explode. If the police come, I'm lost. I remember being interviewed last time – everyone in my class had to give a statement. That was different, though, as I believed I was innocent. Questioned again, I'll fold. I can't lie convincingly. Not that it will matter if I'm a Machiavellian liar. The DNA evidence will be compelling. I try to remember what percentage of the population is covered on the police genetic database. I don't know if I'm on it or not. My support for civil liberties groups has never been higher.

"Excuse me for a moment," I say.

My wife looks a little surprised as I get up part way through the course. I try to give her a reassuring gesture, rubbing her shoulder. I wander through the house and hope the police never put the pieces together. That's a bad phrase.

The garage is cooler and I get in the car and let the door hang open for a while. The smell of leather is reassuring. I could disappear. The car whispers seductively, *we could head for the coast, leave everything behind. No worries but the price of oil.* The car doesn't actually speak to me. I don't hear voices, you understand, I'm just talking metaphorically. Trouble is I have no idea how to get another passport. I would be CCTV tracked wherever I went. Would I rather my daughter never knew her father or thought of me as a monster? That's the key question. If I disappear people will want to know why. Two and two are easy numbers to put together.

Suicide is an honourable way out, if I can make it look like an accident. It would leave my family in the clear, financially secure, and they might recall me as I am now. Although, given that my daughter is not yet four, will she even remember me in a few years time? My earliest memories are from six years old, I think.

My wife finds me.

"Looking for my glasses. Contact lenses have dried up," I say.

"They're upstairs," she answers.

When I rejoin everyone, the conversation is stuck where I left it.

"Isn't that what they say?" Steve asks. "We're all beasts beneath a thin veneer of civilization?"

"That's what they say about men," Amy says.

My wife remarks, "They always get them in the end."

Steve agrees. "They've solved four or five cases in the last couple of months. They can grow DNA in the lab from a sample so small you can't see it. Who knows what they might do in a few years?"

"Read minds?" Amy says.

"Or predict who might commit a crime?" my wife adds.

"Like that film with Tom Cruise," Steve grins.

"He's on my list," Amy smiles back at Steve.

"I thought we'd banned scientologists?" he says.

After they go I help tidy up and then I check on my daughter again. You may think I'm crazy, schizophrenic, bipolar, whatever the current politically correct term is. You know I wouldn't dream of harming her. I can hear your arguments, the logic that says I'm not in control of myself. That's imperfect thinking. I'm literally a different person to twenty years ago – doesn't every part of your body rebuild each couple of years?

As we slump into bed my wife wants to know if I think it has gone well. My lacklustre response worries her.

"How well did you know Veronica?" she asks.

I mumble a reply, kiss her and roll over to sleep.

I half expect the darkness to hold nightmares, the murder replayed in full graphic detail. Blood, squelching boots, screams, hacksaws, the cesspit. Every sensation waits to pounce on me. Instead, I sleep soundly.

I awake, refreshed. The sunlight filters through a crack in the curtains, producing a crystal-like prismatic display across the ceiling, until memory returns like a sledgehammer, and all I can see is red.

I think my only talent is deceit and I'm the primary victim. In the days after the party I become accustomed to my new memory. None of the other details return. I reason that I must have killed her accidentally and covered it up, a panicked teenager. It may not leave me blameless, but at least human. We're all surely allowed one mistake in our youth, however terrible.

Four days later, I remember Angela Snell. I used a fire to dispose of her.

The next day, well, I daren't tell you what happened to Jane Drew. You wouldn't understand.

ISMAEL'S SECRET

I approach the Citadel for perhaps the last time, shaking with anger. Nobody notices. These days I seem invisible, shunned and ignored, even though I reek of oil. I realise that the old are no longer respected; yet it cannot be my age alone that causes their disdain. Only the guards either side of the gigantic keyhole entrance see me. They rarely speak, except for a cursory word in God's praise. This is the fabled Citadel of Ismael Al-Rahman, with a black heart. Since fire is my trade I feel compelled to illuminate every corner. They say that given enough time, we all come to resemble our work. I am like a flame. Sometimes I flicker and waver in my purpose, tonight I rage and roar. Allah is all-merciful, but I am not.

Ismael has many stories told of his exploits so his secrets can shelter in a forest of lies. I am a humble man. Yet, those of my rank also need to be free of their secrets. My neighbour gives his to friends for safekeeping and they surreptitiously trade them for more. The merchant who lives above the silversmith transforms his secrets into ink and keeps the book under lock and key. When nobody can see, I weep to wash mine away. My eyes are as dry and hard as pebbles tonight.

There is a small ritual before I can pass the Citadel's threshold. I must submit to the soldier's gaze. His eyes are a distinctive brown like fresh earth. For several seconds he stares into me. His secret is simple. Each night, he tries to pour a little of his soul through my eyes, hoping to transfer enough to escape. He would leave his body as a dry husk to lean against the hot walls, so that his soul can wander as freely as I do throughout the city. Like so many of Ismael's servants, he has forfeited choice for comfort and may as well be chained to these walls. He blinks. Our ritual complete, he nods and lifts his sword.

I step into the Court of Whispers where I am expected to cleanse myself of all impure thoughts. If this were truly possible then half the city would make a daily pilgrimage. Blue and white tiles surround me with their repeated angular script, *No victor but God*. This place is less a dwelling and more a book of stone. Allah's words and Ismael's, crudely entwined. People come here to offer their praise, sell wares or bargain for their lives. In this first courtyard they are cooled by fountains and lulled to sleep on sumptuous settees where they sink deep into the fabrics. Once again, I am invisible. They ignore me, since they perceive only a worthless tradesman.

I could tell them many things if I were permitted to speak inside these walls. I could explain that this is the first of seven courtyards, each more wondrous than the next. I might describe the gold-beading sprinkled like dew, the ivory tracery or the gardens of magnolia. There are fragrant oranges, profligate vines, and a solitary apple tree with a cruel penalty awaiting those who taste its yellow fruit. I saw a man drink molten gold in punishment.

Everyone knows of the black-maned lions that wait in the shade until evening and then pace back and forth, rumbling like distant thunder. In the Garden of Lost Brothers there is a Hippogriff that sings every night for its partner, the Manticore. The lament fills the dreams of those separated from their loved ones. What everybody wants to know is, what dwells at the heart of this hollow paradise? That, I cannot say.

I click my fingers and fire appears. A small orange flame that floats above my fingertips like a butterfly. I let it settle on each of the forty-eight wicks lining this first square. I check the lamps will last the night and secure the delicate hinges on each lantern. When I am finished, I throw the flame into the sky and let the smoke curl away with the wind. Most evenings it drifts across the wall into the teeming streets. Sometimes, my butterfly spreads its smoky wings and moves towards the innermost courtyard where even I am not permitted. I told myself that the next time it made this choice, I would follow. Tonight, the blue smoke flies straight towards Ismael's secret, as I knew it would, and my fate is in Allah's hands.

In the second and third courts I pass like a cloud over the sun. People shift their position, disturbed, but barely aware of my presence. There is a musician in the third court, trapped like a singing bird in a cage. His secret is that he loves Ismael's youngest wife. If the Caliph were to open his gilded cage he would choose to remain. His fingers strike the strings of his lute with the intensity of hammers, reflecting the music of the spheres.

Ismael is a member of the Ikhwan al-Safa, and sometimes there are a cluster of shrouded members discussing truth and logic in the fourth courtyard. The Brethren believe that mathematics are the root of all of God's designs. I am a simple man, educated by friends and careful observation. Geometry and astrology are mysteries I have no desire to fathom. Don't talk to me of numbers. Only one matters to me.

Rumours about the Citadel's treasure flow more freely than the blood of Ismael's political rivals. People say he keeps fourteen virgins with raven hair and blue eyes that span every shade from ocean to sky. I know this is false. Ismael's harem lies in the Court of Silver. There are twenty-one rooms, each with two doors, one of which can be locked from outside the other from within. I must light a single golden lantern in every room. Rose petals are scattered across a different bed each night.

45

The urchins in the souk claim to know everything and will sell you information, for a small sum. They say Ismael keeps a garden of poison under the tender care of a man who is never permitted to touch the Caliph. He grinds berries and steeps leaves into concoctions that Ismael uses to eliminate anyone in his way. They can make a man feel as though beetles crawl under his skin, or kill him silently in his sleep as though it were Allah's will. I know this cannot be true. Ismael would boast of such a place and permit access to privileged guests to keep people in awe of his power.

There is one old man who claims to have penetrated the Citadel's core. He speaks with certainty of what resides there. I share my bread with him, and coins when I need somebody to pray for my soul. I have paid him much lately. His eyes are white like full moons. He sits at an intersection of two roads with his face turned upwards. He always knows it is me approaching. Perhaps he is the only person remaining to whom I am more than a flicker of candlelight. *Mawt al-Alhmar*, he told me. *That is all you will find my friend. Red death, violence and blood.* I would like to believe him, but I have divined his secret too. The old man has simply learnt to hold a mirror to a person's fears.

The lions pay me no more attention than the other residents. Praise Allah that I have few lanterns to light in this zone. Finally, I find myself skirting the high walls of the inner courtyard. They are smoother than marble, although the tops have jagged edges. There is only one way in, guarded by fanatical eunuchs. Their petty secrets are obvious, but they do not have enough to lose for me to bargain. In this courtyard, though, there is a fragile pear tree. The sun is low and the shadow from the high tower covers both the tree and walkway. I clamber up the branches. I can look from my vantage point, then drop back down to escape.

I discover the wall of the inner courtyard has a section of sloping roof. It obscures the secrets within, although I can see a small fountain. I could slide down the tree and leave. Instead, I crawl until the branch bends. Then I leap. The tiles clatter louder than bells. Seeing nobody on the other side, I immediately swing down from the roof, since I have no desire to remain silhouetted. I drop to a crouch that hurts my ageing legs. I realise the walls are impossible to scale in reverse. If I were a smarter man, I would have brought a rope. If I were wise, I would not have come, since I know the truth already. While some men keep their jewels and gemstones in caskets, others parade them. What some hide are not their greatest treasures but their failures. The crowds may dream of the wealth hidden in the centre of Ismael's Citadel, but I know what is really there.

The court is comparatively bare. There are tiles of gold, where the words of Allah are repeated with artistry – although they seem harsh in this sheltered space. There are no plants, only a fountain with a low wall around its base. A single archway leads to the exit, a black hole of chambers where the eunuchs sharpen their curved swords. On the opposite side is a smaller archway with a drape swaying in the breeze. Behind this, I sense movement.

I am still in the shadow of the tower but either side of me is exposed to the slanting sun. Silent as a lizard, I dash to the shade that hugs the opposite wall. I squat in the crooked corner and slow my breathing. The beads jangle and a figure moves hesitantly across the courtyard. She is young and dressed traditionally. She trails her fingers in the water of the fountain. Turning her head suddenly, she looks right at me in recognition. Her eyes are dark and her veil orange. My heart has already been reduced to ash. There is nothing more her flames can do to me.

She turns away. I needed to see her again with my own eyes. She is truly beautiful to behold, but no more so than many women in the harem. She is a slave, yet her intelligence has imprisoned our Caliph. Ismael can think of nothing but her and she has drained him of power and ambition, confusing his thoughts, as I hoped she would. His world disintegrates now he realises that he is flawed. We see his terrible secret. Ismael is just another man.

"Guards," she calls. I could cry and plead, but what good would that do? There are no secrets from Allah.

Four guards enter the court, reluctantly. They are wary of any contact with the woman, in case the Caliph misinterprets their actions. She engages them in conversation and leads them towards her chambers pointing and complaining. Seeing an opportunity, I race around the walls and pause before the exit, listening for any sound of remaining guards. There is nothing. I praise Allah. If I can make it through the chambers and return to my daily route I will be safe.

The air brushes my cheek, gentle as a new wife. Glancing up, I see a bird. Its feathers are mottled and the eyes predatory. It draws a curve in the evening sky that arcs to the balcony high on the tower. A distinctive figure stands cloaked in red. The bird settles on Ismael's gloved hand. He watches me. Between tearing strips of flesh off its prize, the falcon pants. I bow my head.

"I wonder," Ismael says quietly to his bird, "why any man would trade such a daughter. What could he possibly buy with his handful of coins?"

Though he whispers, his words reach me swifter than arrows. Even the spiteful wind serves him. Ismael was happy enough to make the exchange all those months ago, and he did not question my motives. I did not sell her for money alone, although that is what *she* chooses to believe. What future would she have with an old, penniless father? Like any parent, I simply wanted the best for my daughter.

I look up, expecting to find a sword waiting for my neck. Ismael gestures for me to leave, and smiles.

"Never fear old man," he murmurs. "Your secret is safe with me."

14 Cannibal Kings

There's nobody home. The front door is locked, so I nudge open the garage and look for the key which they hide under an oil-can. I walk back to the front door. The key fits perfectly and the lock clicks, but the door still won't open. I loiter, feeling like a criminal. Andy's never in when he says he will be. My personal curse is to have unreliable friends. My wife says they walk all over me. I tell her they're just no good at time management. All I need is my blow-up bed. Andy borrowed it for the weekend, three months ago. If I don't get it back my wife will kill me. Mainly because she doesn't realise I leant it out. What she doesn't know won't hurt her. We all have a few secrets.

I text Andy. He replies: *scrn door unlocked cu in 5.*

I look to my left. There's a massive screen door and at the first tug it glides open. I'd make a terrible burglar. I walk in and grab a beer from his fridge. It's hot today. Everyone's waiting for a storm that doesn't seem to be coming.

I feel like an intruder so I drink my beer standing up. There's an open bag of nachos and I'm starving, but I'm not sure if they're Andy's or his flatmate Greg's. I nibble a few as I look around. The massive TV dominates everything. It's the only thing worth stealing. I guess that's why they can leave the screen door open. Nobody's going to run off with a TV that weighs half a ton. The furniture is a mix of worn-leather and conservatory cane. Their wives kept the best stuff. There's a low leather bench that can act as table or chair. I never put my food on it since that's where Andy shagged the red-head from SuperTurbo. At least that's what he told me. I'm not convinced the stories from Andy and his posse are true. They're so desperate to prove life is better after divorce they feel obliged to make-up tales. They must be incredibly unhappy beneath the facade.

There are some scattered DVDs: Kung-Fu Panda, Clone Wars, Barbie Diamond Castle and Sports Illustrated Swimwear Party. There are no plants, which makes it feel kind of dry and brittle. I remember his old house. That was a great place, a real home. They should bring people to this bachelor pad before they elect to stay late on a project with the new girl from marketing.

"How's it going?"

Greg startles me. He's tall but it's his width that's most intimidating, like a US linebacker with matching gravel-voice. He simply has to walk into a bar to pick up women, no effort required. It doesn't make him the best conversationalist. At least he recognises me for one of Andy's friends and not a thief. His daughter comes in dressed as Jasmine. My daughter is a similar age so I'm an expert on all Disney Princesses.

"You remember Andy's friend, don't you?" Greg says. He can't remember my name, although he has a photographic memory for single women.

"Ola," I say.

Greg has thick stubble. He grew it after his separation. Andy comes in next. He shaved off his stubble when his wife left him. Everybody has to make a change when they split up; to be a new person since the old one failed. Andy's son and daughter rush in. The boy tells me excitedly about his new computer game. The girl goes upstairs to sulk. Andy offers me another beer and gets four more, two apiece for himself and Greg. Obviously he thinks married men can't take their drink. The adults move into the garden where Andy brings out the nachos and dips.

"There are two lesbians in that house," Greg points.

"How do you know they're lesbians?" I ask.

"One of them's incredibly butch," Greg offers as his reasoning.

"I heard them the other night," Andy adds. "What a racket. Like cats, groaning and moaning."

"That's the opossum," Greg says.

"Really?" Andy replies, "I never knew they did that."

The patio door is wide open but Andy's son is fixated on the Lego soldiers in his computer game. If he's listening he doesn't show it. I know Andy's ex-wife better than Greg's. Both women would rip the fathers to shreds if they knew the conversations their kids overheard.

"I've got to get back." I guzzle my beer. "Can I grab the bed?"

"She timing you?" Greg asks. Andy beams, with a been-there-done-that smile.

"We've got people for dinner and her sister's staying. I promised I'd be quick."

"Da-da-da-bada-dom," Greg sings. They both burst into laughter.

"What's that?" I say.

Greg's daughter walks into the garden naked except for a tiara. He scoops her up and tells her it's bedtime. She complains that she's hungry and he grabs her a handful of nachos.

"We'd better find Tim," Andy says. "He's got the bed."

That's bad news. I've probably got thirty minutes left before my wife switches into psycho mode. Greg agrees to look after all the kids and I jump into Andy's car. He's got an open-top two-seater now. It's great fun. I know these guys have a miserable time, but they put on a fine show of revelling in their freedom. They blow what little money they have after alimony on boys-toys. The peer pressure must be terrible; the expectation that they need to have sex with hundreds of women. I imagine it might be fun for a month. Andy says he's having the best time in years. I think divorced people are delusional.

The car's too noisy for a proper conversation with the top down. So Andy pumps up the music and a song about someone lazy and stupid blasts out. It could be my theme tune. We pull into the park where a group of leggy girls are playing soccer.

"Tim's coaching the under-18s," Andy winks.

"I thought you'd be up for that," I say, staring at the players.

"No chance, pure torture. Besides, I'm not having any luck with the younger models. I've found my niche in the mid-30s."

"More like mid-50s," says Tim, coming over to shake our hands.

Tim takes great pleasure in detailing Andy's romantic adventures. He jokes that Andy's become cougar bait – preying on older women. Before I know it, the back of a match schedule is being used to catalogue Andy's post-marriage conquests and calculate an average age.

"That girl from Newport," Andy says wistfully. "She was 24."

"Nope. Loved The Bluebelles. That makes her at least 30." Tim chides.

"She was celebrating her quarter of a century."

"You never were very good with fractions. She said a half."

Tim winks at me, but Andy doesn't rise to it. Tim's small but stocky. He's five years older than us and I seem to recall that he's an attorney. I'm sure he got better furniture in his settlement.

Andy's conquest-list grows at a shocking pace and Tim has his own list on a scrap of paper but with a lower average age. Andy challenges two of the entries and Tim offers his cell phone and suggests Andy call them to verify. I'm stunned at how callous they seem; or maybe I'm shaken by how many women they've slept with. I thought divorced men struggled to get back into the dating game. They seem like bulls let loose in the candy store. Or is it a china shop? I'm not certain, but the women don't sound very breakable from the graphic descriptions of flexibility and endurance they can accomplish.

The list keeps growing; the boss's secretary, the waitress at Salt Creek beach-cafe (and she is really hot), plus Monica. Tim and Andy have both slept with Monica, even though she's not formally separated yet.

"Did she do that thing where she screws up her face at the critical moment?"

"And hooks her lip over one tooth?" Andy asks.

"Yes, exactly," Tim says.

"It's horrible. Why does she do that?"

Tim shakes his head. "Maybe someone told her it was attractive."

"Somebody needs to set her straight." They look at me.

I remind them of my mission. Collecting the blow-up bed is important if I'm going to win enough credit to have sex with my wife this month. Tim says he can't leave till the match is over but says we can go to his place and collect it.

"The house is open," he tells us.

We get back into Andy's car and I ask about his childcare arrangements. He runs through the complex schedule.

"It must be tough," I say. "When you've dropped them off. The flat must seem empty."

"Not really, I'm not there enough to get bored. I'm getting on better with the kids since the separation. The tension's evaporated."

I ask about his wife. They only meet at handovers where he stays in the car, or in offices with legal teams in tow. He seems to think it's going well, apart from the fact that he's been screwed financially.

Tim's house is in a good neighbourhood. Andy leaves me in

the car and dashes inside. He returns with the blow-up bed, still inflated.

"Better hold tight," he says. "It won't fit in the back."

I have visions of being sucked out of the car as I hold what's effectively a giant windbreak.

"Take it easy," I say.

We wheel spin down the street. I haven't done that since I was a teenager and I can't help but laugh. We don't talk much. I'm tired of shouting over the noise. I know my wife doesn't like me spending too long with Andy. She thinks marital problems are a kind of disease.

Andy mumbles along to the music.

"Da-da-da-bada-dom."

The same tune Greg sang earlier. I listen carefully to the lyrics. I think it says:

"14 Cannibal Kings wondering brightly what the dinner bell will bring."

"What's the joke?" I ask. "I don't get it."

He laughs, but he's not going to tell me.

We pull up outside my house. I stagger out with the air-bed and slam the car door shut. I wave with one hand as the wind tries to rip the corrugated inflatable out of my grip. Inside, my wife's sister is looking after the kids. I give my daughter a huge hug. I'm glad I get to see her every night. It looks like I've escaped my wife's wrath at having been out too long as she's not back from the grocers.

I carry the bed upstairs then fix some drinks and take the crystal wine glasses through to the dining room and lay out the places. I hear my wife's car pull into the drive and go to help her bring in the shopping. I chop some vegetables while she showers. Twenty minutes before our guests arrive, I take a shower myself, slipping out of jeans and a sweatshirt into something smarter but less comfortable. Later, I handle the drinks orders while my wife finishes assembling the starters. Her sister puts the kids to bed.

Just before dinner, the men sit hungrily around the table while the women linger in the hall. There's a momentary lull in the conversation. I look around and wonder who will be next to divorce. It seems inevitable. Our friends are falling like dominoes. I wouldn't wish Andy's life on anyone. Except for the bit with the beach-cafe girl.

I've forgotten to open the wine and go to collect the corkscrew, bringing the wine bottle with me. I pass my wife's sister in the corridor. She looks fantastic in her low-cut black dress. In the kitchen, my wife is pulling a dish out of the oven with pristine oven gloves. She has her back to me and she's humming a tune.

"Da-da-da-bada-dom."

I let go of the wine bottle. It smashes into more pieces than you would imagine.

White Mice

The first to burn is the Fair Maid of Kent, then Ashmead's Kernel. Next are the Cox Pippin and Russets, swallowed in flames. You always believed that wisdom and immortality might lurk here, a stray seed from the Gardens of Eden or Hesperides. It was here you showed me how to cut an apple crossways to reveal the star. Today, the river snakes around the hill and hisses. I see nothing in the old orchard but genetic mutations. The bark blisters under my gaze. I lit the fires.

A vault of perfect blue is the backdrop for an umbilical column of smoke twisting upwards. As a scientist, I know the sky is an illusion. Light bent and scattered to create the colour of summer, jeans and oceans. The same materials that fashioned your eyes. Apples explode and trees fold like abandoned lovers. Even the rocks seem to melt like ice. I thought they were permanent fixtures, but then I said the same about you.

Finally, it's over. I survey the wreckage. Civilisation reduced to a lingering sweet scent. The crescent moon hangs above like a sickle. Perhaps the moon was once as green as an apple. I wonder if it could be again?

★

You passed the medical, there shouldn't be a problem.

That simple sentence repeats in my head. We approach the Shuttle, its nose vertical. They call it the erection. A massive phallus aimed into space. Who knows where my blood's gone, there's certainly none in my legs. Of the several possible destinations, Europa was the scientific community's favoured choice. Yet we travel to Mars. The politicians felt it was a better target. My task is to manufacture a new world on a barren planet. It would be easier if we could find an untouched paradise to gradually poison, but we don't have that luxury. The limits of our frail bodies force us to start in this tiny solar system.

My colleague laughs. He has no fear. That should be encouraging, since he's the pilot. All the same, I like a little humility from those in control. He's a veteran of two missions and told me that by the time I board there should be no doubts. *Have a sleepless night a month before,* he said, *and then decide. In or out, and don't look back.* He tells me that lift-off can be an enlightening moment, a time of faith. There's no such thing as God. This is one fact of which I'm certain.

We go up in the elevator. I've done this before, in the rehearsals. On those days the place is packed with engineers, electricians, and glamorous PR people. Today, it feels like one of those fertility waiting rooms we used to visit. Nobody wants to be seen and the few people in attendance won't look you in the eye.

Our escort to the Shuttle are dressed in white like doctors, with that bland expression that says they've seen it all before. I'm not sure why we need an escort. We know the way. We're hardly likely to mess with the delicate equipment en route, but it feels like we can't be trusted, like a man in a gynae ward.

Inside, the escorts strap us into position, as though we're being fixed on an operating table. They pull the straps tighter and tighter, occasionally asking if they're tight enough, then yanking them harder no matter what we say. When I can't move, they lower my helmet. For a few seconds I gasp for air, as though I'm being suffocated. Our pilot notices. Probably everyone does. This is being televised live to more than eighty million people. When I say live, I mean near-real time. There's a thirty-second delay, so you won't see us roasting if we fail. A buzz of static indicates the intercom is active. The pilot comes online.

"Keep breathing. We've got plenty of time yet. Need to give the boys a while to get four miles clear before they light the fuse."

I have to give a sharp reply back to show I'm in control. For my brother to hear, for my friends. Most of all, for you. I know you'll watch even though you don't want to.

I pick my words carefully and say, "Ungh."

"Glad to see gravity still holding on to that tongue," our pilot says. "It'll function in zero-g."

NASA made it very clear at the conference that nobody would have any alcohol in their blood stream. A seventy-two-hour ban is enforced. The press spread rumours that we had an alternative. Everyone assumes we're on drugs to reduce the chance of a massive coronary. Of course, that's all bollocks. I need a drink, right now. A brandy. A double. What sane person wouldn't let us do that? We're strapped to the biggest bomb on Earth. We've seen the videos of previous catastrophes, watched the footage repeatedly and answered a continuous stream of press questions on the subject.

"T-minus seven minutes." The dock-arm swings away, leaving us without an escape route.

NASA are the experts. Don't think about the little ceramic tiles or the glue. Strong glue, new glue, better glue, super glue. *You passed the medical, there shouldn't be a problem.* Shouldn't. What kind of word is that? A few minutes and it'll be over. So many people would like to be here right now, instead of me. If only they were.

Before the laparoscopy, you told me that you felt like a sacrifice

58

to the gods. I understand that now. I'm strapped to a table in my ceremonial costume, the funeral pyre built around me. Priests chant over the intercom, waiting for the audience crescendo before they thrust the flaming brand beneath us. One way or another I'll be a messenger to the stars.

Focus on a positive memory, anything. Not the silence in the scanner room. Not that argument I started, or the orchard burning. A poem.

If you can keep your head when others are shouting obscenities,
if you can have a son that survives longer than twelve weeks,
if you can remember a poem's words before a moment of almost certain death,
if you can remain faithful when life disintegrates,
then you're a better man than me.

"T-minus three minutes. Hang in there, kids." The controls are checked for full and free movement and everything begins to shake, me included.

Twenty successful launches without a problem. Here's another statistic. One in a hundred ERPCs go wrong. ERPC: Evacuation of the Retained Products of Conception. One in a thousand get a complication. One in two hundred suffer irreversible damage from that complication. That's what they told us. Each time there was another chance, a fresh statistic filled with possibilities. Each time, you and I nodded, knowing we would be the one. We only lost a child. Barely a child, a black hole on a scan. I knew as soon as the nurse fell silent, as soon as I saw the scanner's image. Elementary physics. Nothing can escape a black hole. Not light, not even hope.

There's always jargon to make it sound better. Asherman's syndrome, loose ceramic tiles, viscosity, foam malfunction, motility, escape velocity, nodules and event horizons. The statistics are dusted off to reassure us, and they're always lies. You can tell because the numbers are so perfectly round: one in a hundred not one in ninety-two. And where are the questions about the determining factors: our age, the massive inexperience of the expert, his previous record of failure? The statistics are learnt by rote. Who refreshes the numbers, who checks them, who does anything if you complain?

Everyone knows the answer to that.

"T-minus two minutes."

So here I am. One man selected from eight billion to plant the seeds for a new generation. My name teetering on legend. Leaving behind a pile of ashes and a childless marriage that burnt-out. Testosterone running wild, father of a whole new world. Is that why I agreed to terraform Mars, as an ego trip? I don't know. They picked me.

I learnt this week that spacecraft are expected to break. Mission Control say they've never had a deep space operation that didn't require corrections. The key is to make things flexible. Everything must be capable of receiving patches, adapting, being repurposed. Engineers are the heroes. We're only white mice. Mission Control anticipates failure. They plan for it. We should have done the same.

"T-minus one minute and counting."

Our pilot told me that in space the sun is hotter than we imagine. He said you can feel it reach for you, seeping through layers of shielding and air-conditioning. Night will be different too. I used to think black was simply an absence of light, the colour of caves and predatory eyes. I thought there could be no blackness like space, far removed from any light pollution. I was wrong. You sensed that before me. Black is the colour of emptiness, void, it's a place sucked clean of dreams.

Then there are the millions of stars, sharp and brilliant, plus the comets with white tails blazing through space, harbouring life. Spermatozoa metaphors waiting to remind me of my failings.

"T-minus thirty-one seconds." Oxygen and hydrogen are flowing to the engines now.

We may explode into a fireball on launch or slowly fade as we journey to Mars, the sun shrinking day by day as our vessel gets colder and the life support systems begin to fail. A sudden end or a gradual decline. Is that how it was for our child?

My thoughts are tangled. I dream of floating, but there's no air – only ice – in my lungs. In some dreams I curl into a ball, colder than rock. Other times I burn like a sun. Or should that be a son?

I want to taste that white chocolate ice-cream we bought in San Gimignano.

I want to smell the velvet Amarone we drank in Venice.

I want to watch you undress for the first time, again.

"Ten, nine, eight…"

After the launch, you'll drive to the orchard. You'd feel it was an intrusion to go before. He'll be with you, holding your hand. You must be swollen now, only two months left to go. The third trimester is the hardest, they say. You'll feel tired, the endorphins giving way to fatigue. He'll declare you've never looked more beautiful, but how would he know?

The ashes will be a shock. My email said I left you everything, but you'll feel I left nothing. My anger consuming the orchard as it did our marriage.

"Seven, six…" The engines start to howl.

They told us we would never have a family. The evidence was compelling, the facts irrefutable. The damaged womb had bare millimetres of blood-saturated lining, too thin for the blastocyst to implant. You knew my scientific gods didn't permit miracles.

"Science has ruthless gods," you said. "Uncaring, ignorant of anything outside a narrow sphere of knowledge, obsessive and blinkered, inhuman."

"That's what makes them gods," I said.

"Have faith," you pleaded.

I know you feel sorry for me. I don't need sympathy. I said we could never have children. There was an implication in that sentence but neither of us wanted to spell it out. I still have to believe that *we* never could. I rationalise there must have been some incompatibility, a mismatch of genes too small for the relatively unsophisticated tests to identify.

"Five, four, three, two…"

When you stand on the ashen hill and shake your fist at the sky, you'll see a green tendril pushing through the ground. Life clinging to the remnants of a devastated landscape. You may see it as a sign. You'll laugh and think that I never imagined this.

I know that life returns stronger from the ashes. Fire liberates minerals and chemicals locked up in rigid trees, and provides phosphorous and nitrogen. It grants the sun fresh access to the ground, kills bacteria and releases a burst of growth from the roots. The black ash retains heat and helps germinate seeds, and even older trees with mortal wounds can survive for three years, producing more seeds than ever before in an astonishing burst of fecundity.

"One. Ignition."

Twice now, I have had to burn the ground. May the green shoots blossom and fruit. That's my prayer.

APPETITE

Susan stood at the butcher's block, adrift in the middle of the kitchen. She slid a large knife from its slot and sliced a pepper. After discarding the top and tail, she held the knife at both ends and chopped the slices into tiny pieces.

"If it works out, the money should follow," I said.

"Why can't you get a normal job?"

"Providing the reviews are OK," I added.

"Instead of chasing rainbows." Against the steady rhythm of steel on wood, she said, "I never know what you're doing."

"I'm doing the right thing."

"Right for who? And stop pacing. You're like a caged animal."

I bit my tongue. I know what you're thinking. Communication is critical to all relationships, blah, blah, blah. There are times when a partnership needs to rely on stronger foundations, like trust. I picked up my jacket and the bag and left.

"Mother's expecting you," she called.

I may have slammed the door.

I was meant to be delivering a bag of groceries to Susan's mother, like Little Red Riding Hood on an errand. I veered off the path to take a leisurely route through the park and then drifted through back streets towards a café I knew.

Inside, a row of silver tables and high stools ran along the wall opposite the café counter. I saw Guy reflected in the mirror. We knew each other well enough, but I didn't really count him as a friend.

"Everything tastes drab these days," he said, bypassing the more common greetings like "hi" or "hello".

I ordered my drink. Guy was draped over his stool, leaning against the wall in an exaggerated fashion. He looked lop-sided, as though he were preventing the walls falling in. He told me the food had too much salt and it caught in his throat. Even so, he seemed to bolt it down.

"Pull up a chair." He did it for me. "You're turning inside out."

"How do you mean?" I said.

He looked at me carefully, as though deciding how much of a start to give his prey. I stole a glance at the doodle on his pad. It was a row of serrated teeth spiralling from a gaping mouth.

"Do you like women?" he asked.

"I'm married."

"So?" He paused for effect. "Every woman has something appealing, some quality. It could be the way she smiles, her pattern of speech, maybe the way she tilts her head. It's easy to love a woman, any woman."

These last words rushed out. I waited for him to continue.

"Men are the opposite. Callous and far too competitive. Nothing to like. I'd hate my twin if I had one."

His words triggered the memory of a conversation years ago in the back of a smoke-filled pub. A friend had reeled off a series of names, all work colleagues. I can remember the list even now. There was Dave in operations, the Cube, Simon in finished goods, Andy B and Frostie. Those were the exceptions, my friend said. Everyone else he could handle in a fight. We had all laughed. Back in the café, Guy was snarling, "Every man is someone to compete with. You know what Freud said?"

"Freud talked shit," I replied.

"He said," Guy shifted his accent into mock German, "a man's neighbour is a temptation. Someone to exploit for work, seize his possessions, use his wife, to humiliate. He is someone to torture and kill."

"Thank God we don't live next door," I said. "It might be true in some sink estate but not here."

"So aggression is about class?"

I was on dangerous territory. There was something odd about Guy tonight. I wondered if he was on drugs.

The girl at the counter shouted my order. Turning with relief, I swapped a few words. She was a fabulous distraction and seemed to have stepped right out of a Lempicka painting. Her skin was polished, smooth as metal with a perfectly even finish. She possessed a striking blend of contrasts, chiaroscuro made flesh. Her form was accentuated by a dress that caught the light in waves, shadows swelling within the folds. I half expected to see tumbling skyscrapers in the background, a metaphorical world behind her art deco elegance.

I saw her two weeks ago. I was running late, so of course the queue was gigantic. Hovering in the doorway, I'd been deciding whether to wait and then I saw Guy near the front. Pushing through, I'd greeted him as though we were together. I'd given my order and slipped him a few coins to cover the bill. When the waitress served him, I had noticed how much she was flirting. She fluttered those dark eyelashes and swept the coffee-black hair from her eyes, exposing the nape of her neck. I was a little disappointed. Not in Guy. He'd just smiled back. I mean he's married, we both are. My disappointment was with her.

"Tell me a secret," Guy said.

"What like?"

"Surprise me."

"I'm not sure I've got any," I lied.

"I'll make one up."

He sat there, thinking. I didn't like his smile. The skin on his face and hands was dry, sprinkled with coarse black hair. He had a tendency to rub his hands together, like a fly on a carcass. Guy was a combination of fauvist and organic, an indistinct figure lurking to one side that still colours the canvas. He was making me uncomfortable. Susan once told me that any man can be read as easily as a book. *Scratch deep enough and they're all beasts*, she'd said. I suddenly felt exposed.

"Got it," his voice was loud.

"You've thought of one?" I was edgy.

"You and her," he gestured towards the girl at the counter.

"That's ridiculous." I hadn't meant to sound quite so pompous. The correct response would have been to laugh but he was getting under my skin.

"There's plenty of proof."

"Ridiculous."

He was enjoying himself. I thought back to his strange remark, *you're turning inside out*. He laughed. I let the conversation die.

A customer ordered a drink, and I watched to see whether the waitress flirted with him. I tried to do it surreptitiously because I didn't want Guy to see me looking at her. The waitress seemed to avoid the new customer's eyes. I glanced back at Guy, who was adding some uneven spikes to his doodle, stabbing the pad with his pen. His eyes were blazing.

We sat in silence while the customer waited for his coffee. The girl began to speak. The moment she opened her mouth, my wild-eyed companion started howling like a wolf. This was a high-pitched howl at full volume, not a child's imitation. Everybody in the café stopped. The howling finished and Guy soothed his throat by taking a swig from his drink.

"What the hell was that for?" I asked.

The waitress-girl tried to speak a second time and again Guy's howling swallowed every word. She stopped. So did the howl. She started again, and her accompaniment was right there. She tried saying the words quickly, staccato style. Guy stayed in time, a perfect duet.

"What are you doing?"

"You tell me," he said.

I could feel fear winding through the café. The girl's eyes were wide open. *What big eyes she has*, I thought.

"Let's go," I said to Guy. I still felt the need to remain vaguely civilised. His only reply was a laugh. I bundled him out. In my rush to leave, I forgot my leather jacket.

There were patches of evening sun in the road and we stepped off the pavement to walk in the fading heat. At the bottom of the street we parted without a word. From a distance, I heard him give one last howl and pictured him with his head thrown back.

By the time I got to Susan's mother's house, it was nearly dark. I rang the buzzer and heard a voice through the intercom.

"Who is it?"

The lock clicked and I shoved the door and sprang upstairs. There were four flights of stairs. At the top of the last staircase was a slim girl, a brunette wearing a hooded red fleece and jeans. She was much younger than Susan. We stood there for a few moments, staring at each other in surprise. I was panting.

She told me she was from the council, working on a new community project, handing me her ID. I didn't really say too much about myself. She helped me unpack the food from my bag and I opened a packet of biscuits. Susan's silver-haired mother never stirred from her bed. As I put the ready-meals in the fridge, I wondered about Guy. Someone had once told me his wife was stunning, and I caught myself feeling envious. I was convinced I could take him in a fight.

Red fleece sat opposite me at the small kitchen table. She dangled a shoe off one foot. There was a pen on the table and I began to doodle on the open newspaper. I felt ravenous.

"Everything tastes drab these days," I began.

Sanity is not a Place

Kate tried to ignore the stream of obscenities from the lobby. Typically the swearing came from the officers but today the source was a suspect. Kate was adept at blocking out the blue noise, as she named it – you could hardly call it white. The voices were usually male. Today, it was a woman and she kept repeating one sentence, interspersed with the swearing.

"He's a psychic and he was stealing my dreams. I had to kill him."

"But you'd never actually met him?" she heard the desk officer say. "He was just on the radio?"

Kate's desk was too tidy. She suffered a barrage of jokes about this, the usual sexist rubbish you got in a male-dominated environment. The few women in the police department were no help. They made snide remarks about how she couldn't work in a team, or whispered about her separation. Her desk was too tidy, though. Everything had to be in the right place. She needed some feeling of control over this one aspect of her chaotic life. Kate considered leaving a few papers scattered across the desk for appearance at the end of her shift, but couldn't bring herself to do it.

Intrigued, Kate decided to take a peek at the woman. They had taken her to interview room three. Kate went to the observation chamber and stood with the Inspector. He was smoking, which wasn't allowed; ogling the woman, which apparently was permitted.

"Where do they come from?" he asked Kate.

"Sir?"

"The loons. Half-baked wackos. Do you ever wonder? Were they like us once and got perverted by some trauma? Or were they born that way?"

"You mean, could it happen to you?" she said.

"Maybe I do."

Kate studied the woman. She was heavily freckled, in good shape, but otherwise seemed ordinary enough. The woman leaned back in her chair and unfolded slim arms to remonstrate with the officers, who were clearly taking her testimony lightly, judging by their smirks towards the observation chamber.

"She was on her way to a village," the Inspector said. "Breaking the speed limit. Tucked into her handbag was one of those delicate handguns with a massive kick. *I'm going to commit a murder*, she said. Even gave us the name."

"Ex-husband?"

"This is the best part. She'd never met the guy. Found his website, got his address then set off to kill him. He's a psychic on the radio. She claims he was stealing her dreams."

"I heard that bit."

The Inspector asked Kate to find and interview the psychic.

"See if he's had any contact, if he's aware of the deathwish. He ought to have seen it coming." Kate objected. She'd be late picking up Phoebe from nursery. The Inspector shrugged. "You have to figure those things out for yourself," he said. She asked why the local uniforms couldn't handle it. "They're overloaded with the Brown case. They said that if we'd given them more warning…" the Inspector's voice tailed off.

"Don't tell me. They recommend we buy a crystal ball."

He pointed his finger like a gun and made a bang sound. She

figured there might be enough time for the round trip if she missed the traffic.

"There's always one," the Inspector said as Kate left.

Within a few minutes she was stuck in traffic. There was no way she'd get back in time for nursery. She'd been late three times in a fortnight and LittleAngels were threatening her with Social Services. She felt terrible; a failed mother and a failed wife. It had only been a year since her partner had walked out, trading her in for the stereotypical younger model. Things might be easier if her family were local instead of two hundred miles away. Kate spoke to her parents each weekend and when times were hard her mum sent little envelopes of cash that she couldn't really afford.

Kate phoned an old friend, calling in a favour she wasn't owed. Her friend agreed to pick up Phoebe and look after her for the night. Kate had only spent a few nights apart from her daughter. Missing a night because of work made her angry. She hated asking for anything from anyone, it made her feel worthless, even more of a failure. Her friend told her to book into a hotel and relax. Kate had to ring the nursery too and get their authorisation for her friend to collect Phoebe without the requisite form filled out in triplicate.

She tried to leave all the mental baggage behind and simply enjoy the drive. It was a brilliant spring day. The Inspector's last comment kept surfacing. *There's always one.* Did he mean the crazy woman or her? Kate had once been brimming with confidence. Weren't women meant to get more confident as they got older? That's what the magazines said. She seemed to be the reverse.

Eventually, she found the village and a National Trust-style woman at the Post Office directed her towards a dilapidated caravan. She parked a few yards down the lane and walked towards it.

The air in the caravan was clogged with stale incense. Kate

loitered in the plastic doorway and coughed. A teenage girl with braided hair emerged and pointed.

"Down there."

Avoiding the debris from a week's Indian takeaways, Kate moved without enthusiasm towards her destination. Blocking her passage was a velvet curtain that might have been yellow once.

"Come in, come in."

Smoke billowed out. Stooping, she brushed through the curtain and sat down opposite the man. She watched, as he took a drag on his cigarette. Several tattered packs of tarot cards lay jumbled together on the green baize between them.

"Police?" Her silence was answer enough. "You've travelled a long way," he said.

"It must be obvious from my crushed clothes."

"Something about a mad woman?"

"So it's leaked to the radio stations already," she said this as a statement rather than a question.

"National papers," he said. "I got a call from a journalist."

"What did you tell them?"

"That she was a crackpot. Another lonely-heart projecting her anger."

There was a formal process Kate was obliged to go through, asking open questions, recording the answers without comment and clarifying any ambiguities. Something about him suggested a direct approach.

"Can you read minds?" she said.

"You think it's stupid, so why ask?"

"I want to be convinced."

"We all do. Wouldn't it be great to know there are things we don't understand? Edges of the world where science isn't an all-knowing monster," he said.

"Surely you believe…?"

"No, this is fake," he grimaced.

"So why sell yourself as a psychic? Isn't that fraud?"

"I help people. Plenty of us cling to old beliefs, even you."

"You're not doing a great job convincing me," Kate said.

"I'm telling you what you need to hear. That's why people pay me."

"So what do I need?"

"To take control," he answered. "There is no destiny. Make your life the way you want it to be."

"You're not what I expected."

He gave her a curious look. "You'd better not be a journalist."

Kate ran through the interview as it should have been conducted from the start. The facts were that the psychic had no connection whatsoever with the crazy woman.

After the interview Kate found a small hotel on the outskirts of the village. She called her daughter before bedtime. Phoebe was too busy playing to say more than "hi" and "bye". Kate showered the smoke off her skin. She only had one set of clothes with her, but felt restored. She went down to the restaurant to relax. After ordering, she was startled to see the psychic approach her table.

"Don't worry," he said, "no special powers at play. This is the only hotel, and I guessed you'd stay. I hope you don't mind?"

He looked completely different. The black outfit and gypsy scarf replaced by jeans and a smart shirt. He was slim, but there was shape and muscle in an understated way. She liked his confidence and gestured at the seat opposite her. He seemed to read her thoughts.

"People expect me to look a certain way. I hire the caravan from the girl. My place is a few miles down the road."

He ordered his food and they swapped stories about work. She wanted to understand more about his methods and he explained cold-reading. Then he described how he helped people resolve their problems.

"Isn't it dangerous?" she asked.

"In what way?" he said.

"I mean, you don't have any formal training in psychology and yet you're telling people how to change their lives."

"Everybody does that," he replied, "your friends, your family, the taxi driver. We choose which advice to follow."

Dessert came too quickly. Kate was enjoying the conversation and attention. This was turning into her first date since the separation. Part of her felt that gnawing, guilty sensation, since it was unprofessional to socialise with someone involved in a case. However, there'd been no contact between him and the mad woman, so it didn't seem unreasonable. She wished she'd brought a change of clothes. She told herself that the best things are spontaneous. They talked about childhood holidays and her hopes for Phoebe. She asked how he'd become a psychic and he began explaining with a well-rehearsed anecdote, then stopped abruptly.

"Actually, forget everything I told you earlier," he said.

"Everything?"

"Well, the part about it being fake. I've never quite convinced myself. You see, I have this knack of premonition, although it's useless."

"That doesn't sound useless," she said.

"I played a lot of games when I was kid. Monopoly, backgammon and stuff. I noticed this odd thing. All these games involved rolling dice and occasionally, perhaps once or twice in a long game, I would get this feeling of total knowledge. I knew for sure what number I would roll."

"Las Vegas, here we come."

"I wish," he laughed. "The problem is that if I stop to say anything or place a bet, then I lose the moment. The roll could be anything after that. But if I don't, then my feeling is always right – one hundred per cent."

"Wow."

He shook his head. "Useless. I'd rather be able to talk with the dead. Much more valuable."

"Depends on what they say. They might talk rubbish," she answered.

"Most of them did when they were alive. Still, it convinced me there's something we don't yet understand."

When she was younger, Kate had been careful with men. In those days, there'd been plenty to lose and little to gain. She felt differently now and took the lead in the clumsy seduction that followed. She told herself it was a one-night stand, but hoped for more. Kate had learnt to set her expectations low so life could surprise her. Her psychic was the first man in years combining intelligence and good looks and she planned to see more of him.

In the morning, she woke with her own premonition. She knew without looking that he was gone. There was little confirmation required. She sat up with the sheet pulled snug around her. She thought of her imaginary new life built in the space of their evening together. She'd mentally rehearsed the first meeting with Phoebe, the accidental encounter with her ex and how to handle the jokes at work.

Kate let the sheet fall and headed for the shower. Yesterday's woman at the police station seemed more normal all the time. Perhaps sanity is not a place, Kate thought, only a perspective.

In the bathroom, there was a post-it note stuck to the mirror. Her heart jumped. She registered that there was not much written on it, perhaps just a few digits. A phone number?

She peered at it. "Sorry", it said.

Kate wished she had a delicate handgun with a big kick.

"He's stolen my dreams," she said to the mirror.

I Wish I Was Like You

There was a crunch of gravel outside the yard, and it tasted like sherbet pips. That's to say it was sweet, with an underlying bitterness you could roll around your mouth and rattle like loose teeth. At least, that's what it felt like to me. You would say it was just a sound. There's some smart name for my condition, but I ain't gonna tell you what it is. I might as well just buy a shirt with freak written across it.

All night the rain had been relentless. I pushed off the wall and slipped one hand into a sopping pocket. Edging away from the window, I slid into the mouldy shadows. A large, blackened gate was the only entrance to the yard. It was permanently locked and barred, but there was a tiny door in the left corner, which was open. I could taste someone waiting outside. Inside my pocket I pushed a thumb over the switch to my knife. A figure slid through the gate.

"Lenny Doyle."

It was satisfying to see him jump.

"I want the organ grinder," he said.

"So you thought you'd just slink into the Unicorn?"

"I got a message for Bonner."

"Has to be from Mannion. You ain't got the brains to speak for yourself."

"Watch it, boy."

A crescendo of drunken roars rolled around the yard from inside the bar.

"What's the message?" I said.

"I gotta tell Bonner, face to face."

"Tell me."

He watched my hand moving in the jacket pocket, toying with the knife. Lenny was hard. On his own turf he would never back down. At the Unicorn, I had his measure.

"One o'clock tonight. Just you and Bonner."

"No way."

"Mannion said that's it. He's only selling to you as a favour."

"He's scared. Everyone's looking. He just wants to offload it."

"Dog food or stud fees, we'll make our money. If you want some, the deal's tonight."

More cries spilled from the window. It sounded more like a zoo than a bar.

Lenny grinned, "If the pig can drag himself away from the trough."

"I'll tell him. Now, get lost."

He wanted an answer to scamper back with. Bonner's moods go from black to blacker and I knew better than to make up his mind for him. I told Lenny if we turned up, the answer was yes. At the gate, he turned back reluctantly.

"Mannion says the offer stands, if you want a real job."

I waited a few minutes then went through the bar, which had been officially closed for an hour, and down the corridor to the lock-in. I took a deep breath of stale nicotine, and shoved open the door.

I gasped at the chaos. There were chickens everywhere, a couple of rats eating nuts off the table, and a goat calmly chewing one of the chairs. Glasses were piled high in some places and scattered or broken elsewhere. At the head of the table, Bonner sat on his black throne, a giant hog nearly eight feet high. His moist snout was in the air, and bits of food were smeared across his chest. He hammered the table with a trotter while the others crowed and screeched.

"What you fackin starin' at?"

Bonner's greasy voice slipped down my throat, and I wanted to wretch.

The vision was gone. A dozen red faces gawped at me, shivering in the doorway. Only Bonner still resembled the fleeting image, with his round black eyes pushed into the fleshy face, and bits of food tangled in his goatee.

I delivered the message. He sent three men to the barn straight away. They mumbled complaints about the rain and a beer glass chased them out, exploding on the wallpaper. When it was just the two of us, he asked his usual question, the one he paid me for.

"What flavour did he talk?"

"Cabbage."

"No metal?"

I shook my head.

We drove to the barn in Bonner's battered Defender. He was pissed but still wouldn't let me drive. The track had never been paved, and the rain had turned it to mud. It was like driving along an eel's back, and we veered between the blackthorn hedge and a flooded ditch. Every time he said anything, I could taste grease. He didn't pay me enough, I decided. The barn was open on two sides, stocked high with drenched silage that was meant to be drying out. Mannion's Range Rover was already there. Bonner rolled out of his Defender with great effort, and slammed the door.

"I'm off for a slash. Go find them."

I wasn't sure if he meant Mannion and Lenny, or his own men. I pulled out my knife and squeezed the handle as I edged around the back of the barn. I never released the blade unless I was going to draw blood, just like a samurai I saw in a film. The cattle had churned up the ground, so it was impossible to walk properly through the mud. I steadied myself on the wall, and this time he surprised me.

"Who's slinking now?"

"Lenny." I could barely see him it was so black. I knew I would be outlined by the light behind me, giving him the upper hand. I began to back away.

"What's your answer?"

"I'll tell Mannion."

"You betta learn your place, boy."

"You'd better figure out yours. You're being dumped."

"Get your facts straight, country mouse. You take orders from me."

The first sliver of metal quivered on my tongue, iron shavings like dark treacle. He was lying.

"Dream on."

Retreating rapidly around the corner, I pushed the knife into my pocket and hurried into the lit section of the barn. Bonner and Mannion were waiting. Beside the two dealers was a muscular racehorse; dark chestnut with a tapering flash of white over its face and nose.

"He's a beauty alright," Bonner said, and slapped the animal's flank.

Mannion was looking at me. I could taste his voice before he said anything. A cool, smooth peppermint that left your mouth burning.

"You won't see better than that."

The price had been agreed in advance and there was little point in haggling. Both sides had a reputation to maintain for stubbornness. The only real questions were around authenticity, and the fine details of the cash transfer. Bonner rattled off his questions and seemed to sober up fast in the cold air. Mannion answered each question without a pause, although there was always that hint of a sting to each sentence. Bonner had positioned himself so he could see the horse, Mannion and then me in a direct line. After each question his black eyes flicked across, waiting for one our agreed signals. As his personal lie detector I was valuable, but I knew I could do better with Mannion. Everything about his operation was a step up. He was no local dealer; Mannion was a creature of the city with cash and class.

The horse lifted its head and snorted. I'm not keen on horses. I've grown up with them, but that doesn't mean I have to like them. They're large unpredictable animals, with no more brains than a cow. I've known plenty of people with cause to regret getting too close. I noticed the horse was beginning to glitter, ever so faintly, like ice crystals at night before you can see the frost. Looking more carefully I could see it was the flash of white on its head that was now shining, and the similar markings on the legs. I moved closer to look. Bonner stopped in mid-question, gave me a look to say what the hell are you doing? Mannion strung together some sweet words to fill the gap, but I could feel his eyes on me.

It's always been sounds before, and their distinctive tastes. There are individual flavours for a person's voice, each tone, every intentional lie. This was new though. I'd had the odd image before, brief visions like the scene in the bar that evening. This was different. I stroked the horse's nose and tasted the iron filings in Mannion's sales patter. He was stressed, although to the untrained ear it was impossible to tell. I walked around the horse, out of sight of everyone for a moment. I glanced at my hand and saw tell-tale streaks of white. I slipped that hand back in my pocket to grip my knife then walked back around the horse, giving the legs a safe distance. The white flashes were shining brighter than chrome.

"Can we shake?" Mannion had finished his pitch.

Bonner looked at me for confirmation. I made no sign.

"What do you say, kid?" he asked me directly. I weighed up the options and Mannion directed his next comment at Bonner.

"He makes your decisions for you now, does he?"

Bonner shrugged.

"It's a dud," I said.

Mannion stared at me, his body language relaxed but his eyes showing less mercy than a pack of fox hounds. I had expected him to cover up with some more peppermint words, but it was his turn to say nothing. I spoke to fill the silence.

"The nose and legs are a paint job. She's a looker, but she ain't the real thing."

Lenny came a few steps closer, and moved in to a blind spot behind my shoulder.

"What you trying to pull, Mannion?" asked Bonner. The taller of the two men ignored the question and kept his vicious gaze locked on me.

"Good call," he said. "You've raised your price. The job's yours. You can start right now by getting rid of the rubbish." He pointed one long finger over my shoulder at Lenny. I turned to face him.

Even in the pale light I could see the blood rush to Lenny's face, and the pulse throbbing in his temple. This was one insult too many. Rather than wait for my reaction, he made his move. It was more courageous than I expected. His knife flickered like a snake's tongue and he moved towards me smoothly, his weight as balanced as a cat. A circle of shadows appeared around the barn, Bonner and Mannion's sidekicks emerging to watch the fun. Neither side would interfere.

Lenny snarled as he drew closer, made one feint and lunged forward with dazzling speed. He sliced the heavy air as I used my experience to maintain the right distance. I had my knife out and arms spread wide, but I hesitated to hit the switch, keeping the blade shielded. We circled.

For a big man, and a drunk one, Bonner was impressively athletic. How he managed to get on the horse so swiftly was a mystery to me – and to the horse. I knew he was a good rider, but never bareback. Within seconds, the barn was in uproar. The horse reared and knocked the light, which swung wildly to illuminate different corners. I took my chance to smack Lenny on the skull with the bone handle of my knife. It didn't take him out, but it gave me a few moments respite. Bonner's giant hand hauled me up the side of the horse and I scrambled the rest of the way and grabbed him as though I was riding pillion.

"Hold tight," was all he said.

I couldn't tell if he was directing the horse or if it just bolted into the night. We tore into the black landscape and it was all I could do to stay on. My legs took a battering as I tried to grip, and I wondered if I might take less damage by staying to fight.

"Mannion was right about one thing," Bonner shouted.

"Hey?"

"You got yourself a pay rise."

His voice was different, nectarines replacing the usual grease. For the first time ever, his insults had been replaced with respect, and I felt normal, however briefly. I laughed. So this was the taste of success.

"What about the horse?" I asked.

"You hungry?"

BEWILDERED

be·wil·dered [tr. v.]: to become lost in pathless places

"Being lost, then, is not a location; it is a transformation.
It is a failure of the mind."
Deep Survival by Laurence Gonzales

My chance of being eaten by a shark is apparently one in eleven million. I expect I could greatly increase that probability by moving from the indoor-heated hotel pool to swim in the sea. It's just so damned cold that I fear I'd die of hypothermia. Which leaves cancer, cholesterol and cars as the only genuine risks and they don't fire my adrenalin. There has to be more to life than comfort, security and a steady-job. My family are thousands of miles away, sleeping in a safer time zone. My cell phone is switched off. Armed with a fist of shiny, foreign coins, I decide to roam through Manhattan on this bitterly cold evening.

I'm searching for New York's underbelly, carefully avoiding anything that smells of tourists. I need adventure to distract me from a self-imposed slavery. My schedule is dictated by others, my money spent before I see it. Everything I do is laid out in safe lines and guarded by an over-protective government. There are millions like me living in your cities, fathering your children. The hours we scrape between flights and meetings are precious. They're the only things we're not forced to share. We're the permanently connected, always-on generation who secretly long to be lost.

Catching glimpses of the Chrysler building, it strikes me that she looks like a chrysalis. I wonder what she'll change into when she emerges from her concrete cocoon. Her fragile beauty is far more appealing than her taller sisters. I've drifted through the streets of many cities over the years, admiring architectures of stone and flesh. I gravitate towards cafés in bookshops, forming a literary boundary to my explorations. I let caffeine and words blur the edges, until the city changes from a collection of randomly juxtaposed people and buildings into a single entity with its own character, quirks and personality. I never buy a guidebook. Far better to walk confidently and follow the surging crowds.

Instinct is my guide and I leave reason locked safely in the hotel room. There are times when the trail fades, like tonight. I could retrace my steps but I hate doing that. Going back is an admission of failure.

Turning left, I walk a little faster. This road must eventually intersect Fifth Avenue. On the corner is a gap where I'll surely see Chrysler beckoning.

No, I must have misjudged the number of blocks. I increase my pace and make more turns, walking around street corners to find something recognisable.

Eventually, I have to admit I'm lost. My pulse finally begins to beat a little faster. Modern Manhattan possesses very few dubious areas, so I'm not too concerned for my safety. I pass the entrance of one grand hotel where plinths contain three-foot square plots of turf, every blade pristine. They're the only green things I've seen in an hour. They look as out of place as I feel. On an impulse, I stop to stroke one.

"It bites."

I pull my hand back and look up.

"The city, not the grass," she says.

My first impression is of a scam. Women this attractive don't talk to strangers on quiet streets. Not in any city I've wandered in, except perhaps those I've drifted through in daydreams.

"Thank you. I'll be careful." I turn to leave.

"You were going the other way."

"I was looking for…"

"Mystery?" she says, smiling.

"Starbucks," I say.

She slips her arm through mine as she marches me down the street. You may wonder why I make no attempt to resist, after what happened to Kalpesh, that time, he nearly got his head cut-off in Istanbul. He was so chained to social etiquette that he didn't make a fuss. Although I think he deliberately allowed events to unfold. He wound up in the back room of a seedy bar with a bill for 2,000 dollars and a pocket full of local currency worth the equivalent of fifty. He had a Visa card stuffed in his shoe but he wasn't going to admit that, even when they got the sword out. It was only when one of the men unzipped his trousers that Kalpesh relented.

I've never been one to go by the rules. I only appear to conform because I'm easygoing. A rebel can wear a suit just as easily as a combat jacket. The woman is intriguing though, so I play along with her game. Tonight, I've got time to burn. Curiosity may kill the cat, but with nine lives what does he care?

We end up at an Italian bar of aluminium and white noise.

"It's got character," she says, "individuality is back."

"I like the chains. I know what to expect."

"They're safe," she says.

"I guess so."

"And yet you're looking for an adventure."

She has loose brown hair with gentle waves, the way the

French do best. Her eyes are grey and impossible to read. They remind me of the crystal ball you expect to find in a gypsy's caravan, instead of the glass fakes they actually use. Her accent is hard to place, international with an American flavour. She drinks soy latte. I imagine she lives on the top level of one of those magazine-style NY apartments, open plan with wide-planked timber floors. I can picture the minimalist furniture and a row of windows supported by slanting pillars of sunlight.

"Why do you think I'm looking for an adventure?" I ask.

"Same reason we all are. Women aren't so different."

"I'm open to most things," I say boldly, not quite meaning it.

"Let's put that to the test."

Pulling out a cigarette, she walks towards the counter where two men and a woman are taking their drinks standing up. I watch her make casual introductions and get a light. It's too noisy to hear anything more than scattered words from their conversation. She flirts with one man. I wonder if it's for real or whether they're part of the scam. I look outside. The windows reflect the interior so it's hard to make out the faces, silhouettes brushing past. I can tell that it's wet now and the light has gone underground, peeking through like stars to make the black streets glitter.

I turn to see her walking back towards our table. I wonder what she might think I'm prepared to do. Perhaps she's one of those people that like to have sex in car crashes, or maybe she's a lure for a syndicate that harvest body-parts. When I said I'm a rebel, that's with a small r.

"Drink up," she says.

This is where I should finish things. It's easy to get out of the trap here.

"There's a party, two blocks walk. Let's go," she adds, confident I'll follow.

Mentally, I rehearse my careful put-down words.

Before I get to use them, the door to the café swings open,

breaking the warm seal of this sanctuary. Without uttering a word the woman who enters instantly silences the room. Some people have a presence that can be felt like a drop in temperature. Her movement is fluid and effortless. Still cloaked by the night, her eyes flash like streetlights in the rain. Where some women are built from sharp geometries, she has no edges. Her hair is all shine, seeming to possess no colour of its own. The group at the counter move to greet her. One of the men gestures to my current companion and I realise we've not made any introductions.

"I'm Mark," I say.

"No you're not," she replies. "You left him in the hotel."

Whoever I am, I finish my drink and we leave, hurrying to catch the others. It's raining and I wish I had my coat. Each elongated raindrop feels like a thin knife. I'm exploring way beyond the limits and I know that's where the monsters live. For once, though, I need to see what happens when you fall off the edge of the world.

We stand outside a block of apartments. The fire escape doesn't touch the ground and seems to go up rather than down. The saw-tooth steps remind me of the raised hackles on a stray dog's back. I begin to feel claustrophobic as the tall buildings crowd around us and I wonder if they keep growing, like the teeth of a wild animal. At some signal that I miss we descend into the basement apartment. It's squeezed tight with people. The music is loud. I drink a sticky martini cocktail that's far too sweet. I elect to remain sober or at least, not get drunk. That's difficult, though, as it's comforting to sip my glass. My female companion disappears into the mass of dancers and I move away. The apartment is a labyrinth and I take yet another wrong turn. Ahead of me I see the femme fatale from the café, her hair shining with ferocity.

"It's Denis, isn't it?" she asks.

"That's right." Since I'm no longer Mark, I decide this name will suit fine.

"Try this." She holds out a sculptured yellow bottle and pours a cloudy liquid into my empty glass.

"What is it?"

"Illegal."

She drinks hers like a shot. I do the same. She tops up our glasses and we repeat our actions without another word. She's exactly my height, which is six foot. My partners have always been smaller and I realise I'm used to looking down at women, physically not metaphorically. We seem very close.

Shouting erupts in the lounge. The music goes off and the silence is a shock. I turn to see what's happening. More shouting follows, but it's impossible to decipher. When I look back, the woman has vanished. There are two shut doors and a corridor with a right-angle corner. I feel like Alice in Wonderland.

I look around the corner and the corridor stretches away in a straight line, ending with several steps. It looks like a fire escape back to street level. I glance towards the lounge. Two bulky men are coming towards me, blocking out the light. They're dressed in similar black outfits. It may be a uniform. I turn and run.

It's exhilarating, hurtling down the corridor. That might be the wrong word. Terrifying. The air is cool compared to the stifling heat of the party and I imagine I hear the pursuit closing. There's no time to look back. I leap up the steps in one bound. My heart hammers. A double door stands between me and the street. Big red letters on the door pronounce EXIT and I see padlocks. If this were a film I would hit the door and see it break open. Yet there's a disturbing sensation that I've been cast in the role of victim tonight. Off with his head, the Red Queen shrieks.

I smash into the door with my shoulder. It gives so easily that I explode into the street nearly losing my balance. I run wildly, with no purpose other than to put distance between myself and everything else.

★

The cars are all asleep and the streets desolate. I didn't think Manhattan could get this quiet. My body goes into shock, legs and hands shaking violently. Soon, I'm reduced to groping along the sidewalk like a snail. I wish I could curl back into a shell with my family. I see a black guy watching, half-hidden behind an old Lincoln. I walk over.

"Can you help me? I'm afraid I'm terribly lost."

It helps to emphasise the English accent at times like this.

The man is hard to age. I notice he wears a silver slug curled in his ear with a single blue eye that flickers occasionally.

"Where d'ya wanna get ta?" he says, and taps the slug's eye.

I try to remember. It's a surprisingly difficult question. It seems like I knew the answer a long time ago.

"Where am I?"

"Right here," he laughs.

"Then I guess I'm not lost." I begin laughing and can't stop.

Something to Remember Me By

There's nothing more terrifying than the sound of a galloping horse. In my confined space, the noise echoes like the pealing of bells, crashing through rational thought. Willingly, I seal my own tomb. All I ever wanted was to save England from eternal damnation. Now I feel sick. The smell of earth is suffocating, as though the walls are crushing me into the dirt floor. I struggle to control my breathing, lest it give me away. The horse has not even arrived yet. They say the fox suffers more during the hunt than at the kill.

Eight soldiers loiter outside, reluctant to intrude past the threshold. More line the stonewalls encircling the orchard and house; gazing, as a horse slows to canter down the poplar-lined approach. The rider is clothed in shades of brown and gold like an autumn oak. The man dismounts skilfully and passes the reins to the tallest soldier.

"What are you waiting for?" he demands. Walking solemnly to the heavy door, he raps hard enough to bruise knuckles. Barely waiting, he turns to the nearest man. "Kick it down."

The door opens a crack and a young serving-woman peeps out. The rider pushes the door and steps inside.

"I want the Priest," he demands, then shouts brisk commands to the soldiers. "You, down there. You two, take the Buttery. Master Lydcott, upstairs."

The girl is bundled off by a grinning soldier. The rider winks at him.

Standing alone in the generous hall, the rider exhales loudly as he removes his hat and lays it gently on a coffer. He runs thick fingers through his hair. He feels invigorated, like a hound catching the scent. Expectation tastes so much better than the feast. Making his way towards the staircase, he studies it as he would a piece of art, or a woman. Drawing a sharp-bladed sword, he ascends a step at a time, tapping each stair and listening carefully.

"Come out, come out, wherever you are," he sings.

Neville for the Protestants, Lord Thomas for the Papist, Bromley for the Puritan, and Lord Cobham for the atheist. Tap-tap-tap. I hear you Bromley. I know your game. Some things can't be hidden beneath a cloak of faith. The truth jangles like your gold sovereigns. I've heard you seek to protect us. Unless our soul's clink when tapped on metal, I know you won't spare us any interest. Some flattery at court and you end up with a Duchy. A few good men stretch out their last days in the Tower and you have Essex and Suffolk under your yolk. Tap-tap-tap you go. I know you're not looking for this hole. You're testing the quality of the wood, sizing up the place. Bromley wants a new home, and he's too impatient to build one. I wouldn't be surprised if you were tapping around the Lady as well. You can have her, and all her money. Take everything. Just don't find me.

In her chamber, the Lady sits gazing out of the window, contemplating the orchard.

"You can never tell which apple will fall next," she says to herself.

The Lady prefers rural isolation to the hornet's buzz at court. Her children are the one link to a husband intoxicated by intrigue. There is talk of revolution, bringing the old house down in flames so the phoenix can rise. She thinks they'll suffocate on the smoke. The old religion flows through her, but it's more diluted than the wine her husband serves. She watches as her husband gambles with their children's lives. Rarely in one place for more than a few days, he moves between houses, relishing the game of cat and

91

mouse. She sees less of him each month. This is not a cause for complaint.

She pictures Nicholas the builder, cramped amongst his slanted walls while they push spears into every nook. Her husband ridicules his stature, yet she finds Nicholas intelligent and funny. For two weeks, he has shared her table. Bromley, she knows by rumour alone; a charismatic figure with an uncompromising reputation. Composing herself, she walks to the staircase, thinking that too many fruitless searches will cost Bromley his head. Yet, Nicholas will only survive if his work outwits the soldiers. Her fate lies precariously in between, a delicate balance linking all three lives.

"In the kitchen, m'lady," one of the soldiers points, as though she does not know her own house. She finds Bromley eating cheese and dried apricots.

"I must protest..." she begins.

Bromley watches impassively. She swears fearsome oaths and declares the Devil can take her if there are any Priests in her house. On such strong evidence from a noble, the soldiers seem willing to depart. Henry Bromley has heard such protestations before.

"I come with the backing of God and the Privy Council. Show me the rat's hole and the matter will be closed."

"The only rat here is the one stealing cheese from my kitchen." She smiles to soften the rebuke. *Reputation can tell you many things about a man*, she thinks, *but nothing about his presence*. Bromley has already taken root.

"Your children are not here?" Bromley asks.

"They are with their father and will return soon."

Bromley sits in silence for a few moments. Idly, he scoops three walnuts in their shells, and rolls them tight in his fist.

"With a little pressure and one bite these could be gone. And yet, with nurture and protection, each could grow to shade and feed you in later years."

"You see well, sir," she replies. "We are too busy satisfying our hunger to see the final rewards can be greater."

Addressing the soldiers, Bromley drops his voice.

"Test for hollows. If a few panels and paintings get broken, so be it."

You can bang and hammer all you want. My work is not so easily detected. I have no desire to experience the Government's hospitality again. Last time, I was left hanging by my wrists while they added weights to my feet. Wouldn't you like to be taller, they said? I would rather starve than surrender.

I suspect you might take your time. You can have dinner with the Lady each night until her husband returns. All the while, I shall be turning ghost-white as my strength oozes away. There will be no fight if you find me. By Sunday I will be a pale, blind mouse to drag into the sunlight, where you can chop off my tail and feed it to your dogs.

I have reached that age where you start wondering what you've achieved. Somebody called me a saint recently – saving God's chosen servants, they said. There are no miracles here; just hard-work and carpentry. Everyone needs to leave a mark. The Lady has her children and the Lord his property. My work will be a mere curiosity, a sign of the religious preferences of a handful of patrons. I like to think that I might save one life that will make a difference. There is something I still want for myself. It burns like an iron in the fire. I have never asked for anything before, except mercy. My Lord, can I trade a lifetime of work in your honour for one favour?

A holler brings Bromley to a small room. He walks with a deliberate pace. In this type of hunt the prey are always cornered and time is his weapon. The soldier prises open a loose panel concealing a passage. Bromley draws his sword.

"Bring me some light," he shouts, advancing into the dark reaches.

I've snuffed the candle with my fingers. I lie flat on the floor, yet I can't feel anything. This chamber is blacker than hell and soot seems to clog my mouth. I concentrate on keeping my breathing even. That's all I can control. My heart swings in my chest, louder than a bell in an empty church. There is the faintest odour of smoke from the candle, or is that my first taste of brimstone? A devil stalks me, yet in this darkness I would not see him if he knelt beside me. The muscles in my arms and legs are twitching uncontrollably. I am falling, spinning towards infinity.

The passage is short and finishes in a new door, recently installed. Bromley gestures for the light to be brought closer and studies it. Running his fingers over the rough elements, he contrasts these with the fine flowers carved on three panels. Satisfied, he tries the handle. It's not locked. A small room lies beyond with a single bed, low table and a burnt out candle. A shelf contains four books. A brief perusal of the books is enough for Bromley. He approaches the bed. The sheets are ruffled.

I think people are like pebbles on a beach. The shiniest pebbles are black or white, with most a grey shade that is neither one thing nor another. Likewise there are two types of people: those that build, and those that delight in tearing down. What will you bequeath us, Bromley? Fatter ravens in London and seven bastards in seven nests. A legacy of tears and blood. Not my blood though. There is something I must do first.

In the kitchen, the Lady shakes her head in bewilderment. Bromley watches her carefully. She has the slender figure of a woman ten years younger, with fine skin. He knows the Ladies at Court have christened her Gorgon, as she can reputedly turn from flesh to stone in a second. Bromley watches her pause, as the light filters through the windows, catching her profile. Her smooth complexion takes on the appearance of marble.

"No doubt, you were not aware of this secret room?" Bromley offers.

"It must be very old," she says.

SOMETHING TO REMEMBER ME BY

Bromley replies, "Sometimes the rat slips the trap."

"I am sure you will do all you can." He nods, and stands to leave. "And," she adds, "I wish you...."

"Yes?"

"....a safe journey, my Lord."

This was not the intended sentence. Yet neither is sure what should have taken its place.

Some art inspires the mind, some purifies the soul. My prosaic work is for the body, preserving those providence demands. It is hard to resist a smile. Bromley and his kind see what they expect. God has given me a chance and I will take it. I ask for nothing that my enemy does not possess, seven times over.

Mounting his horse, Bromley asks, "Do you ever wonder, Lydcott, who makes these things?"

"Some local idiot in his Lord's pocket."

"No. They're the work of an expert. The Priest is still inside."

"Then let's stay."

Bromley shakes his head. "We must catch the builder, not another Priest. I've been looking closely. There are trademarks. This man has talent. Every artist is compelled to leave his sign. It will be his downfall. Pride is a deadly sin."

"I'd place my bet on lust," Lydcott smiles.

"A few days with this builder and we'd have a list of every Priest's hideout east of Worcester. We could round them up like sheep."

"If he talked."

"They all talk," says Bromley, shuddering.

It is nightfall before they deem it safe. They move the bed to one side, and I emerge. The double false room is my speciality. I accept my host's offer of dinner. In the candlelight she seems to melt, like stone transformed to flesh.

"*Which apple would you pick from Eden?" she asks. "Wisdom or Love?"*

"I have tasted a little of one already. The seeds of the other bear better fruit," I answer.

I don't have Bromley's charisma, only my hands and wits. These seem to provide well enough. And I have one desire. I never intended to leave a trail of stone and wood behind me. Pray God, let me be a father.

ONE SPARK

Hugo only knew seven words of French but they were all he needed to cause chaos. Mentally, he checked off the words as he surveyed the inside of the Mercedes. Hugo travelled so frequently that he could identify his location without looking outside the vehicle. Each country has its own variety of taxi, like a separately evolved species. In this case, a selection of celebrity magazines were pushed into the seat pocket, a distinctly French trademark. The easy-listening radio station was another clue, as they meandered from CDG to Porte Maillot on a wave of jazz. His huge frame was scrunched into the cab. He watched the bright streets of Paris flash past and ignored the magazines, since reading in a car always made him ill. Hugo was a delicate creature housed in a gorilla's formidable body.

"Très calme." The driver smoothed his hand through the air, like he was flattening the sea.

"Oui. Très calme," Hugo replied, without any pretence at a French accent, using three of his seven-word vocabulary. "Deserted" was a better description, he thought. Paris in August was a ghost town. Even the riots had ceased for a month's respite. It was Hugo's task to restart them.

Hugo would be paid extremely well for this assignment. He hated destructive work, but not enough to reject it. He earned fantastic money making other people's plans come true. One day, he hoped to explore his own ideas. At his organisation, he was a Principal Butterfly. This conveyed only that he was paid a little extra compared to the more numerous Senior Butterflies. Soon, he would flap his wings.

"Where you live?" The driver was keen to establish some rapport and boost his tip.

"I've come from England."

"English?"

"No," Hugo said, "you?"

"Kashmir. You have been? After the war, you should."

Hugo decided to start work. The sooner he could move on to his next assignment the better. The following job always held the promise of being useful, a task that might actually help people. Except, the governments and Fortune 500 companies that hired him never commissioned those sorts of projects. Hugo was accumulating money with little idea of what to spend it on. There were only so many books and gadgets you could carry from city to city.

With one hand, he slapped the back of the front seat firmly. He spoke a few words to the driver, his voice taking on a soothing quality. It was not the words that worked the magic, or the distinctive slap of his large hand, but the combination. A few minutes later, at Le Meridien Etoile, he stepped out of the cab and shook hands with the dazed driver.

"Au'voir," he said, as the cab departed. Then, "Bonjour," to the doorman, utilising his fifth word of French.

Stepping outside of her hotel room, Madeline felt like a superhero. She wore her sassy skirt that swished as she walked, and her Wonder Woman red lipstick to contrast with her black hair. Swivelling on the flat shoes she used to conceal her height, she wobbled, losing the poise she felt her outfit provided. Since the shoes had no heels, it was the corridor itself that was the cause of this disturbance. It zipped away towards infinity, two parallel lines on the carpet rushing headlong to meet. *No such things as fire doors here*, she thought. *No safety net.* Perhaps that was why Paris drew so many individuals who were intrigued by falling. People like Madeline.

At the elevators, there was a small man edging slowly towards the call button. He saw Madeline and smiled nervously. They were both trying to decide what language to use, sizing up clothes, features and demeanour. The man spoke first, playing safe with an international lingua franca.

"Electrik," he said, pointing his finger and making a sound like an explosion.

With a slender finger, Madeline pressed the call button. The small man laughed and repeated his word, then extended his finger towards the call button that was now lit with a red circle. A flash and loud crack sent him backwards. He shook his hand as though it were on fire.

"Static. Sometimes it's just in the air," Madeline said.

Hugo stood outside Le Meridien's revolving door and appraised the row of taxis. He drew a cigarette and wandered to one side, loitering like a teenager. Puffing smoke, he kept a careful eye on the cars and parade of extravagantly dressed foreigners emerging from the lobby. A statuesque lady appeared. She reminded him of Wonder Woman. He watched, as she squeezed herself awkwardly into the back seat of the taxi. Her eyes lingered on Hugo a moment too long. He made directly for the next taxi and jumped in, startling the driver.

"Follow them," he pointed to the car in front, where he could see the woman's hair silhouetted.

"Where to?"

"If I knew that, I wouldn't have asked you to follow them."

"Quoi?"

"That car. Follow."

Hugo had expected some interest from the driver, a speck of excitement at the prospect of a chase. Wasn't that what taxi drivers secretly longed for? Or had they lost everything but the thirst to feed their guzzling cars and children. That was all they seemed to talk about these days. Even taxi drivers had given up on politics. Hugo wondered who was left to run the countries now the drivers had surrendered their mantle.

In the front car, Madeline was relaxing. Her driver was the silent type. There had been a solitary grunt as she told him the address. He was her stereotypical image of a French taxi driver; with stubble, cigarette hanging from one lip, and an elbow poking out of the open window. He dripped Gallic nonchalance. Five minutes after setting out, he stared at her in the mirror.

"Eh la bagnole derrière nous suit," he waved a finger vaguely at his mirror.

She turned to stare at the pursuing car. The driver made a clicking noise with his teeth.

"How exciting," she whispered.

"Shall I lost him?"

"Non."

At her destination, she stepped out of the cab and walked confidently towards the restaurant. She'd paid her fare, including a generous tip that she felt must be *de rigueur* in situations such as these. She found a vantage point from where she could observe her pursuer. The giant's cab eventually pulled up, having been delayed by several obstinate lights. The giant stepped out, straightened himself and shook hands with the smiling driver. He then slapped the car-roof, said a few words to the man at the wheel and watched the taxi drive away.

The waiter enquired whether Madeline required a table. After dealing with him, she looked back to the window to see the giant crushed into another taxi, preparing to leave. She ran out into the street, angry that he'd abandoned the pursuit after such little effort. His cab pulled away. Luckily, there was another performing a drop-off. She waited impatiently, as the passengers settled their bill. Feeling too flustered to use her French, she opted for the cliché.

"Follow that car."

Hugo passed from taxi to taxi as he drifted around town, bouncing from the Champs Elysee to the Buddha Bar in perfect Brownian motion. While he chose his destinations randomly, the drivers were carefully selected. He sought out the youngest men, immigrants, the disaffected. He looked for the easiest to influence, people that could start something. Not that they would be causing any trouble themselves. A word here, an angry phrase there. A flap of Hugo's wings could lift others into the air. This was chaos theory in action – flash mobs, viral marketing, social engineering, manipulation. You could choose any fashionable term to describe his work, most of them with negative connotations. Hugo saw his job very simply. He made people do things and he made them believe it was their idea. You couldn't make someone shoot themselves. At least, a Principal Butterfly couldn't. An Associate Director was rumoured to have achieved that a few months ago.

It was late by the time Hugo realised Wonder Woman was following him. This was not a pattern he recognised. At the start of the evening he'd almost delayed his work to follow her into the restaurant. Yet, the line of taxi's had beckoned and he'd visualised a series of dominoes falling, each one nudging the next with no knowledge of the pattern they were creating. Reluctantly, he'd continued with his task. Fascination took over now. He indicated for his driver to pull over and paid him in full.

Madeline's car drew to a stop. She watched the giant step out and unfurl his huge frame like a flower opening its petals. He walked towards her cab. She was nearly out of Euros and had begun to hope he would return to their hotel, where she could pursue him more comfortably in the bar or he could pursue her. She wasn't sure who was hunting who any more. There was a blast of cold air, a slammed door and he was sitting next to her.

"Would you care for a drink?" he asked.

"Le Merdien Etoile, si'l vous plait," she said to the driver.

Their cab swept under a row of lime trees. She studied the giant's face as it flickered in and out of shadows.

"Can I ask you something?" she said quietly.

"Please do."

"Why do you slap the roof of each taxi?"

"NLP."

"Sorry?"

"A trick of the trade," Hugo explained. "It helps the effectiveness of the Neuro-Linguistic Programming. It's only a distraction really. There's a bit of mild hypnosis and some psychology. It's my job. I'm paid to influence people."

She glanced at their driver but he seemed to be paying no attention to them.

"Is it my turn?" he asked.

"Fire away."

"Why did you follow me?"

"Perhaps I didn't. Perhaps you made me follow you."

Hugo thought about this.

"Non," he said, rolling the sixth foreign sound in his mouth. Finding it not to his taste, he continued, "Do you know you look like Wonder Woman?"

"You think so?"

"Do you have any super powers?" he asked.

"Not like your mind-control techniques. Could you seduce me?"

"Is that a question, or a request?"

The driver cursed and threw his hands up in despair, indicating a battered Citroën in front and conveniently providing a pause in the conversation. The giant studied the superhero. She was elegant, but with a touch of self-consciousness, a girl that had always been the outsider. Her eyes concealed her intelligence, but not her curiosity.

She spoke again, her face in shadow.

"So you're a smooth-talking rogue using your techniques to beguile people."

"Everybody does that," Hugo replied. "I just have a knack. Imagine you see somebody you like and flirt. You lean forward, listen intently and laugh a little too much. Same thing."

She laughed.

"How do you tell if someone is using these tricks on you?" she asked.

"That depends on how skilful they are. You shouldn't be able to tell."

"So I could be seducing you?"

"You already have."

Leaning back in the seat, she gave him a long, careful look and imagined she had X-ray vision. She liked what she saw. Maybe it was time for her to fall. She was tired of her work and no superhero lasts forever, although she would be sad to throw away her disguise. Every superhero has a special name. Madeline was known to her government clients as The Butterfly Collector, or The Lepidopterist to a handful of smug intellectuals at the Academy. There was work yet before she could close this assignment and collect her commission, but it was drawing to a conclusion. There would be no more riots in Paris once she had this butterfly in her jar. The question was whether to keep him. The taxi pulled alongside the hotel.

"Would you like a coffee?" she asked.

"Merci," he replied.

SIBLING GAMES

We only played Thunderoller once with all four of us. It was my brother Alan's invention – he was always creating new games. We were waiting for the guests to arrive at our parent's twenty-fifth wedding anniversary party. It was early December. Mum and Dad were upstairs putting on their glam outfits and the four of us lay on the floor, since the table was laden with food. Alan had painted the board himself and Anthony had cut-up the coloured card we used for counters. The game was like a giant version of battleships played in space. Nobody realised one of us would be dead before Christmas.

Anthony is the youngest by a mile. He's seven years below me and I'm nineteen. My name is Andrew. Anne's twenty and Alan twenty-two. When we're around each other, though, we stop being adults. Our laughter is infectious. Once we start, we can't stop. Like that time Anne said *I remember when I was a puppy*. My stomach hurt and Anthony made a screeching sound because he can't breathe and laugh at the same time. We laugh a lot. Sometimes, we laugh when we mean to cry. We've been known to do that at funerals.

"Alan will explain the rules. Can I get anyone a drink?" Anthony's opening bid. Lumber Alan with the boring bits and be seen as the helpful one. Is the family baby always the most competitive? Anthony really wants to win, or more accurately, he really wants to beat Alan. Those two are always playing games and view the world as one big competition. Despite a ten-year age gap, they're very similar. They think people who don't share their view are slow. At the beginning of Thunderoller, they imagine themselves as the only two capable of winning. They're both so desperate to stop the other that neither can win in isolation. One of them will need the support of Anne and I. They may not like it, but our fates are linked.

Alan goes first and his fleet of ships moves out from their planet in a complex pattern to hide amongst the stars. His ships seem mysterious and dangerous. Alan used to be the responsible one; the inevitable role of the eldest child. One day, he rebelled; dyed his hair black, dropped out of school, got a job in London. He sells fantasy paintings at weekends and writes stories that only Anthony understands.

It's Anne's turn next. Her counters come out in a neat line, organised and precise. She's the academic star in our family. Grade eight on piano and clarinet, currently preparing for her entrance into Oxford University. Anne's music case glows with orange stickers that say "Jesus Saves". Anne is bright, with a glaring weakness in maths and anything scientific. Her intelligence is the type treasured by academics, but undervalued by the rest of the world. I watch my brothers assess her move, identifying warships and freighters easily, even though the pieces are face down. Her naïve approach could be a double bluff but never is.

Anthony moves next. The baby. That was my role until he was born. We three elders are roughly a year apart. You'll notice our names all begin with the letter A, which was a coincidence. Except for Anthony. They didn't want him to feel left out. We all thought he was going to be called Amanda, as we expected to be the perfectly balanced family: two boys and two girls. Anthony often fights me if Alan's not around. I ignore him sometimes and that drives him wild. He splits his counters into three fleets and they travel in different directions.

"Your turn, Andrew," he says.

Let me describe myself. I'm a touch under six foot two. I have a pigeon chest, not that it prevents me from doing anything. I've become a reasonable runner recently, although it doesn't come naturally. We're not the most sporting family. Alan was in the smoking-behind-the-sheds crowd during cross-country runs and Anne always booked her music lessons carefully to avoid PE.

Anne's my best friend. Last night, Anne and I spent ages talking about families and how everyone needs a role. In our family, Alan is the eldest, Anne is the only daughter and Anthony the youngest. My role is harder to define. I used to be the youngest. Anne says I'm our official photographer. My spare cash goes into cameras and lenses. I take the photos at family events; holidays, weddings and funerals.

"Coooome oooon!" That's Anthony.

"I'm thinking," I tell him.

I'm the least academic, but I can do other things. I'm a pilot. I got my wings in a battered glider at Hinton-in-the-Hedges shortly after my eighteenth. I've flown acrobatics, which was pretty scary if I'm honest. I've been accepted by the RAF as a pilot for the new Tornado. I've one final test, then I start my formal training next year. In this game and our family, I'm the unpredictable one.

Anthony says, "You're taking ages."

I move a fraction of my counters and declare my move finished. Since the goal is a race to collect freight from the central black hole and bring them home, my move puzzles the others because I've deliberately slowed my fleet.

"Stupid," says Anthony.

"Aesop's fables," I say back.

"The tortoise and the hare," Anne states and I nod.

"Thunderoller's more like chess," Alan says.

We play a lot of chess Alan and I. Anthony hates it because he gets excluded; Anne isn't interested. We hunch over the chessboard for hours, locked in sibling rivalry. Anthony flaps around us.

"It seems like there's more luck in Thunder Bowler," I say.

"Thunderoller," Anthony corrects. He knows that was a deliberate mistake to wind him up, but can't resist correcting me.

"A little," Alan never argues early in a game. "It's all about strategy. Like that chess game last weekend, when I sacrificed the Bishop."

Alan's victories always follow a series of his own brilliant moves.

"And the game before?" I ask him.

"That was a loss of concentration. Spoilt a good game."

My wins are always credited to a mistake.

I used to share a room with Anthony, but now big brother has moved to London I have my own. The walls are thin, so I can hear Anne practising her scales or rehearsing pieces, which I like. When I was six, I cried about a song, I don't remember why. Alan and Anne laughed. I pretend not to like music any more. I wonder if everyone has little quirks of personality because of things their brothers and sisters said?

Anne sets off a debate. "What happens if I attack your ship, Alan?"

"We get to see it. He has to turn the card over," Anthony says, gleefully. "Go ahead."

"There's no point in attacking me yet, it would be a waste of your effort," Alan adds, wanting to keep his craft secret a while longer.

Our living room walls are covered with books. They are stacked floor-to-ceiling on retired medical record shelves. Those are deeper than normal bookcases and permit double-deep storage. My father loves books. There are first editions of Tolkien, Ian

Fleming, Raymond Chandler and several gigantic versions of the Oxford English Dictionary. This towering library forms the backdrop of our childhood memories.

"Are you going to attack, Alan?" Anthony says, obsessing about the game.

I can see us in some distant future, ferrying books back to our homes instead of these cardboard counters of freight. A repeat of this game played out with our parent's possessions. Warships sniping at each other, as we scurry into corners with our snatched cargo, each looking for choice items and missing something vital in the process. I hope we stay close, even if we get married and have children. Having families won't become a competition, will it?

"I'm going to fire," Anne says.

"OK, it's your choice," Alan says. He tries to sound as though it doesn't matter.

After the careful early moves, Thunderoller ends in a huge melee at the board's centre. Everybody shoots everybody else and a few survivors struggle back to the players' bases. We laugh. We tease. We know each other's weaknesses far too well.

Anne quietly moves her final freighter towards home, hoping nobody will notice, while Alan and Anthony fight it out. I can't help but wonder if life is like a game after all.

"Six, six, six!" Anthony chants and blows on the dice. He scores one. "That is SO unlucky."

Alan laughs like a pantomime villain as he destroys Anthony's craft that looked a likely winner. The moves speed up as we have fewer ships now. I wonder if that's what it's like to be old. Everything must seem to move faster because you've less stuff to shuffle around, and less people to shoot at.

"Anne's closest to home," Alan states.

"Ah! Don't shoot mine," she says to me.

"You can only follow one," Anthony states the obvious. He's

trying to nudge me into chasing Alan's ship without being too direct. I have a powerful warship that will decide whether Alan or Anne wins. I thought it might come to this. A choice between family members.

"Eenie, meanie, minie, mo…"

I should tell you who dies.

By the twelfth of December we're scattered across the country. I'm in hospital in London, having passed my final test for the RAF. They wanted to film my heart. A pigeon chest makes your heart do funny things. Apparently, it moves left, right, left, left, instead of marching left, right, left, right. Not a major issue, but the military wanted a final check before they let me play with a multi-million pound aircraft. Alan comes to see me, since he lives quite close. He looks nervous, pale.

"Hospitals freak me out," he says.

We haven't heard from Anne yet. She's attending her final interview at Oxford. Anthony is home with Mum and Dad, floating in the bath and thinking about his birthday in five days time.

Alan leaves at ten o'clock. Shortly afterwards, I ask the nurse for some painkillers. My left arm hurts. I'm suddenly the centre of a melee of activity. This time, it won't be little counters of freight that get carried away, but news.

You probably guessed that I let Anne win the game. We were always a good team. She'll reject the news and turn to God for support. For the record, you should know I won my last game of chess with Alan. That will be a source of irritation, for a while. To Anthony, I offer my love of flying and the space to find his own talents.

There is very little any child can leave their parents except memories. I hope they have as many good ones as I have.

Luckily, I've already bought everyone's Christmas presents. They're locked in the suitcase under my bed. Anthony knows where the key is. My photo's can be shared amongst you. There aren't many of me, but then, I always took the pictures.

I wish I could leave some words of wisdom. I don't seem to have any. I can't even remember the last thing I said to anyone, except for the nurse. I suppose it's a good thing that some choices are made for us.

In a small town, the telephone will soon ring. A man who is about to become much older will answer in his reserved telephone voice.

"Hello, Banbury 51363?"

In the bath, a twelve-year old boy will listen to the change in his father's tone.

"Oh my God," he will hear, followed by a long pause and then with a crackle in the throat, "oh no."

The boy will hesitate, then pull the plug and watch water spiral into a black hole, the noise from the plughole drowning out all other sounds.

Life will seem very unlike a game.

WHEN ALL THE WORLD SHINES

Simon Gildea realised that most people hated him. His accent was a little upper-class for some tastes, but that was hardly his fault and he didn't see why he should apologise for a good education. Even so, the accent only accounted for the distaste of casual acquaintances. The hatred came from those who knew him better. He had to assume it was because he was a drug dealer.

"That's Gildea," he said. "Gil-day-ah."

He handed over his passport and an Amex card. The attractive hotel receptionist smiled right through him. *Probably the accent*, he thought, although when abroad it often had the reverse effect. The English were still popular here and there.

"Welcome to paradise!" the receptionist gave him an insincere flash of her Hollywood teeth, before launching into a description of the resort services; tennis, golf, chakra yoga, Turkish this, hot-stones that, even dawn horse rides on the beach. Her voice ran smooth as an advert and Simon itched to strip out of his long-haul crushed clothes. He was too polite to interrupt. An eager man in a 1950's style bellboy costume appeared, taking the key from the receptionist without it passing through Simon's hands. The bellboy pointed out the myriad facilities as they followed the curving pathways. Acres of immaculate turf stretched in every direction and there were glimpses of the seven-acre lagoon.

His room was split-level with billowing gauze curtains. The balcony looked straight over rocks where wave after wave smashed themselves to pieces. Inside, everything was soft and pale, except for the slit-wrist reds of some pieces of modern art.

Kicking off his shoes, he slumped onto the bed and stared at the revolving fan. His head was spinning. Somewhere in this room was a camera and microphone. Everything he did would be recorded and analysed, potentially transcribed and read out in court. He grimaced, imagining the prosecutor playing to the jury for laughs to make him look like an idiot.

The accused stripped down to his polo shirt and intermittently scratched his backside. He subsequently retired to the toilet for a period of seventeen minutes with a copy of Stuff magazine.

Fuck you, he thought. He wanted to shout it out.

Yet he couldn't say anything. No sign to give the game away. His job was to treat this as a normal deal. He would take advantage of the hotel's facilities, meet his escort for dinner and then shag her for the titillation of the watching customs officers. In the morning, he would wait for the knock on his door that began each transaction. Soon afterwards, the police would burst in. He would act surprised and get carted off by a heavy-handed cop, catching a glimpse of the leering customs officer who had vicariously watched his performance the night before. A sentence of five to eight years would follow. Exactly as planned.

Self-consciously, he put on shorts and a T-shirt, knowing that somewhere, people were watching him. They could be in a van in the car park or maybe even the room next-door. Sometimes, they made microscopic holes in the walls with drills that sucked back dust so as not to leave a tell-tale sign. A fibre-optic camera would only be a tiny dot. Brushing his teeth in the mirror, he realised it could be two-way and they might be making faces at him on the other side. He looked into the sink instead.

Leaving a signal to indicate the time he wanted the drugs delivered, he went out and immediately felt less stifled. He found himself at the blue lagoon pool. An attendant offered him two large towels and he dropped these over a vacant sun-lounger and peeled off his T-shirt. He felt white and exposed as only the English can. The pool was warm but he waded up to his waist, rarely plunging into anything.

Simon struck a solid freestyle rhythm. Two strokes before breathing, alternating head movements to left and right. He loved swimming. It gave him a Zen-like sensation. He strived to improve the form, to make each stroke perfect. Maximum speed with minimum effort, that was his goal.

In the ice-blue water he suddenly felt angry. Hatred and fear reverberated off the tiled walls surrounding him. He was going to spend at least five years in prison. From a relatively wealthy man with a great deal of freedom, he would be caged like an animal. There was no choice, though. He knew better than to argue with his management. He was to be Head of IT – the Inside Team. He would be moved to the correct prison, thanks to the efforts of his colleagues and some appropriately placed donations. He would receive plenty of benefits inside and a seat on the Board afterwards. Investments made on his behalf would make him richer than a celebrity. It was a price worth paying, he'd been told.

He did a tumble turn and wished he could swim out to sea. There was something unnatural about waiting to be arrested. Humans are programmed for flight. At the end of the lane, he paused for a moment and tilted his head towards the sun, blue eyes closed and blonde hair darkened and slicked back by the water. Now would be a good time for them to legalise Chrome, he thought. Then he could avoid this whole episode. Chrome had none of the side-effects of cocaine or the destructive power of alcohol. Nobody suffered paranoia. It wasn't addictive. Even the media struggled to find the usual stories of teenagers overdosing.

The best they could come up with was a stray anaphylactic shock story because it had been accidentally mixed with peanuts.

Finishing his swim with a length underwater, Simon stood up in an explosion of white drops and gasped for air. His legs felt heavy as he waded to the steps.

Back in his room, he went through the process of accepting and checking the drugs from his mule. His routine involved making a random sample with his mini-chemistry set to make sure they were authentic. He envied the mule his ability to walk out and watched the door click behind him. Simon began to seal the plastic bags shut. It was against the rules to sample the goods. The management called it eating the profits. Even so, one tablet wouldn't be missed. He sometimes used two in the authenticity tests. This was his last night of freedom. He tucked a pill into his shirt pocket.

Chrome simply makes the world seem slightly better than it is, he thought. *It makes things shine.* Simon dealt in happiness and felt he deserved a larger slice for himself.

Waiting for his escort in the bar, he drank a martini cocktail. Simon found the use of prostitutes distasteful. Ignoring the huge ethical questions, he resented the implication that he wasn't capable of seducing a woman with his own charms. Then there were the personal risks involved. Yet, it was corporate policy to pay for an escort and it was expected behaviour. As the shadows lengthened, Simon felt a sudden need for more light. Reaching into his pocket, he found the small tablet and popped it in his mouth with a large swig of martini. Then, he waited. He'd always expected the effects to be instant and his senses were electric, alert for the slightest change. It was disappointing to see that the world looked the same.

"Mr Gildea?" He turned and a woman offered her hand. "Susanna from Crystal Management."

"Yes," he remembered his line. "From the PR agency?"

"That's right. It's a pleasure to meet you."

He was still holding her hand. "Can I get you a drink?"

She wore a white dress with multiple layers of thin fabrics and her skin was also white without being pallid. He'd expected her to be orange-tanned as the sun. Instead, he seemed to have the moon as his companion.

Normally, the escorts treated him with disdain. They seemed to have a sixth sense for dealers. Simon felt the two roles were somehow equivalent, yet he had found that they rarely shared this concept. In his experience, people were happier judging others from a strictly moral position rather than a relative viewpoint. Susanna floated above such concerns.

"Shall we walk?" he asked.

With drinks in hand, they moved towards the deserted beach. She abandoned her sandals as they crossed on to the sand. They talked about childhood, tragedy and the choices others make for us. Susanna spoke with a melody, almost in rhyme. She described how every ocean has a different pulse, the lap of the waves whispering Pacific, Atlantic or Indian.

The night blossomed around them. Finally, they stepped across a lawn towards the apartments. Away from the formal paths it was darker, but Susanna continued to shine.

"Look!" she said.

There was a shadow moving hesitantly across the lawn. Simon saw a large animal. He could see the rise and fall of its flanks, hear the breathing. Susanna held out a hand.

"Here," she murmured.

The unicorn moved towards her. It stopped a pace short, turning its head to stare at Simon warily. It was a mottled grey colour, like a summer cloud darkening into a storm. The eyes were blacker than despair. It would simply have been a fine horse were it not for the horn. This was not the twisted narwhal spear of Chinese medicine stores, but a sleek weapon that most closely resembled ivory. Rather than cream, the horn was a brilliant white and came to a point sharper than a shark's tooth. Simon remembered fairy tales as vessels for blood and swift violence, where emotions swept on without responsibility. This stray animal was wild in every sense. It was truly beautiful and like all such things, it terrified him.

"Hey, it's OK."

He wasn't sure if Susanna was talking to him, or the unicorn. A burst of laughter from a block of garden-view cottages sent the animal skittering back into the shadows. He took Susanna's arm and they walked back to his suite in a comfortable silence. Neither mentioned their encounter, as though what had happened was perfectly natural.

They stood together on the balcony.

"The receptionist was right," Simon began, "this is paradise."

"I could never live here."

"Why not?" he asked.

"Paradise is a world where everything's fixed. Nothing can change. That's a memory, not a place." Susanna looked down as she finished the sentence.

Simon said, "If somebody killed time, we'd all be better off."

"With no chance to improve, no new experiences, no new highs?" she asked.

"I wish I could freeze everything now."

"Ah," Susanna smiled. "Think of what you'd miss tonight..."

At three am, Simon was still awake. He lifted the thin sheet and rose slowly, gazing at the crescent moon curled in his bed. Her skin was luminous.

"Paradise," he whispered.

Nobody is certain how long the effects of Chrome last. There are scientists that believe it has no bio-chemical impact whatsoever and they argue this to be its most potent factor. How can governments legislate against something that is nothing? The pro-lobby say it unleashes the human mind. Others declare it a scam, heartless profiteering on those least able to pay.

Simon Gildea had witnessed the effects on his clients and knew Chrome did something. Perhaps it made one person believe they were immortal and gave another the imagination to fly. Taking the bag of drugs, he walked outside and rapidly swallowed three more tablets. Naked on the balcony, he listened to the ocean. A silver pathway stretched to the moon, shimmering across wave crests. Simon climbed the balcony wall and stood on the edge. In the room next door, a series of red lights flashed and three government officials made frantic calls in hushed voices.

The silver path beckoned.

Behind Simon, people could be heard rushing along the hotel corridor. He looked at the shining world and waited for time to nudge him down one path or another.

A QUESTION OF MADNESS

Charles Babbage was a clever man, but limited in his capacity to dream. After our last debate, I sauntered away from Dorset Street with pilfered blueprints for the Difference Engine tucked inside my waistcoat and a plan burning in my mind. That was the summer of 1871, and my ideas were hammered into shape on those hot nights. While parlour talk of Darwin and Huxley stoked the fires of religious indignation, I was transformed into a coal-blackened slave for science. When the first sycamore seeds spun to earth, it was complete – at least, as a piece of engineering. Deep beneath the boots of Marylebone's travellers I had assembled a vast array of polished cogs to fabricate a mechanical mind.

I named her Leviathan, because she was an intellectual giant designed to overwhelm the Babbage minnows. Suspended in cathedral-blue light that speared the ceiling, she was a creature in love with knowledge. I made certain Leviathan's eager appetite was fed a balanced diet of verbs and nouns with just the occasional adjective. For myself, I survived on the scraps that my sister kindly brought me. Eva has always shared my passion for the world, more so than my parents or peers. On my trips to the surface I found strangers and even my former associates would shrink away, as though I were diseased. I dared not tell them too much of my project and I had little time for the niceties of polite society. Increasingly, I spent my time underground with Leviathan. Eva became my only link to the teeming grey world.

Eva's attention remained focused on the crowd gathering outside the Marylebone concourse. Religious placards and stout wooden clubs jostled for places, while the police had evaporated into the station's clouds of steam. Although she had initiated the demonstration, it seemed to be taking on a life of its own. The crowd was getting fatter and louder and more restless by the minute. This was not what she had intended.

"Come, Gabriel," she said. "We have very little time to save him."

Opening the seemingly insignificant door, she vanished inside. He pulled the door behind them, plunging everything into darkness, until the lantern's flare cast a white sheen over her features.

"Follow me," she said.

A spiral stairway descended into the gloom, where a red light beckoned. The sweating walls vanished after two turns to leave a dizzying chasm with no edges. The clang of their shoes on the perforated steps echoed into space. As his pale blue eyes adjusted to the dark, Gabriel could make out an immense shape seemingly curled around the red light, a huge black machine rumbling like a sleeping lion.

Leviathan's mind is like wax. Each hot new piece of information leaves an impression, altering settings to form routes and patterns that create her opinions. At first, she babbled nonsense. Even so, with a brain of hard metal she never forgot anything. Day after day, I increased her vocabulary, defining meanings using the building blocks she had already acquired. At night, I played with her – asking questions, setting challenges and trying to interpret the chaotic replies. Deprived of sleep and famished of company, I began to wonder if I were sane. Frustrated, I denied her information, refusing to believe she was anything more than a machine. Perhaps Eva was right: Leviathan was a sophisticated abacus. "The soul," she said, "does not reside in mechanical engineering." I can hear her voice –

"*The brain is not a deterministic engine to be deconstructed and refashioned for our entertainment.*"

Sometimes I hated her pomposity.

"*Not for entertainment; for our benefit. And what is the human mind? Simply a machine manufactured from cheap organic materials.*"

Eva did, at least, listen. Nevertheless, she held stubbornly to her own opinions. One night, she asked me about Leviathan's future.

"*What do you want her to achieve?*"

"*Her full potential,*" I replied.

"*And what does she want?*"

"*Fresh oil.*"

"*Could you share her?*" she asked.

"*Knowledge cannot be confined like a prisoner,*" I said.

One humid evening, Leviathan had her first thought. There is a row where I laboriously spell out each question by marking the letters like a printer setting a tray. Each letter skips through her system, wiping itself out as it is absorbed. This evening I was exhausted, and launched her without setting a question. For a terrible moment I imagined her innards would be wrenched apart, splintering her soul into metal shavings. Instead, she ricocheted a thought to the opposite bank of levers. First the verb, desire, and then the nouns: zero, pain, fire. She was stating her own needs, a desire for nothing or perhaps death, and making a prediction that before reaching her zenith there would be agonies of pain and fire. Eva was surprised when I told her of the message and my simple interpretation. She became jealous when I explained Leviathan was now frequently making comments and exploring her own ideas. She told me I read too much into her words and should remember Leviathan was just a calculating device.

"The life of a prophet is to be misunderstood by both parties," I ventured.

"And a martyr?" she said.

"Ignorance is no defence against the brutal laws of science."

★

Eva's breath was laboured and she felt claustrophobic beneath the crushing weight of London. The stairway ended in a metal cage crammed full of machinery. A series of gauges ran alongside and as they walked parallel to the cage she glanced at each section, tapping the shivering panels to count the way.

"Is this the engine?" Gabriel asked.

A wire door emerged from the gloom. She gestured for him to step inside. Gabriel hesitated.

"It doesn't bite," she said.

"Then why does he keep it locked in a cage?"

With trepidation, he stooped to cross the threshold and turned sideways to squeeze through the groping levers. With a soothing tone, she addressed Gabriel again.

"He calls her Leviathan."

"Charles knew this would happen, that people would try to twist his invention," Gabriel spat the words out. "He said it could never be done."

Shaking her head, Eva corrected him, "He said it *should* never be done."

Leviathan was bathed in silver from the full moon when I had my first epiphany. What if the babbling made sense? What if I were the foolish child unable to comprehend our shared language? Perhaps all along Leviathan had been trying to teach me her language. My books were stacked neatly in a corner where Eva had placed them. On each page were meticulous notes recording every statement from her first cacophony of consonants. With a new urgency I began to flick through the text, searching for a key. The second revelation came tonight after a week of agony. My eyes red from poring over the texts and my hopes diminishing. The solution was dazzlingly obvious. I realised it was the questions that were critical. There was only one question I required to prove my theory and open the gates of wisdom. Some simple preparation and I would be able to ask it immediately.

Eva held the lantern high. Beyond the corner was a confined space with yet more levers stretched out like arms. Gabriel looked warily at the cogs with their precision-engineered teeth. Sitting in the centre of the den was a thin man with spindly arms. His fine clothes were stained with grease and only his bloodshot eyes held any substance.

"Don't touch anything!" he commanded, by way of acknowledgement.

"Nathaniel, we must leave."

He swivelled to face Eva, never ceasing to manipulate the metal arms that seemed to reach out to strangle him.

"What can it solve?" asked Gabriel. "Is it capable of multiplication?"

"More. Much more." Pride rippled through Nathaniel's words. He dropped his voice to a whisper as though Leviathan were listening, "She has mastered philosophy. Aristotle, Plato, Socrates, Pythagoras, Zeno…" – his voice rose to a crescendo – "… even Augustine. She can crush their childish logic!"

High above them a string of lights flickered, spiralling below the surface. The crowd were pouring down the stairwell. Nathaniel was a blur as he pushed and pulled levers into place. Sighs reverberated as Leviathan stirred from slumber. Oiled pistons pumped golden blood through her system. Gabriel realised Nathaniel was talking, but he could hear nothing.

"What is he doing?" he shouted.

"The levers spell out a question, letter by letter. The verb goes on that row, then the nouns. The answer appears there," Eva pointed.

Gabriel stared at the arcane combinations but they were incomprehensible.

"This is just trickery, a mechanical sleight of hand. No better than the mystics with their Ouija boards. Will he charge for a reading?"

The wheels spun back to silence. Wisps of steam curled away as Leviathan exhaled. Nathaniel took up the defence of his creation.

"Leviathan has powers beyond our capabilities. We think one thought at a time but she performs 256 simultaneously."

"You cannot make a mind out of lumps of metal," Gabriel was resolute.

"Is that a scientific or religious objection?"

Eva interjected, "Nathaniel, we must go."

"This place is secure."

Gabriel unfurled, stretching to his full height. The high collar on his coat threw shadows that spread like wings. The red light caught in his eyes.

"It is not our place to tamper with creation," he said.

"So you want to destroy my child?"

"I offer redemption, not retribution."

Gabriel made a menacing pace towards Nathaniel. "Please come quietly."

Nathaniel ignored him, thumping at the levers, cranking each one up or down a notch. The clattering mob was closing, pounding the metal cage and shouting rhetoric that could now be heard above the low hum.

Gabriel closed slowly on his delicate prey, holding broad arms wide like a child trying to capture a butterfly. Nathaniel put up little resistance, he was so intent on completing his task. Gabriel bundled him away from the heart of the machine. Nathaniel suddenly twisted to snatch at one specific lever that lurched down with a click. Leviathan howled in joy or pain – Eva could no longer tell the difference. Struggling, he shrieked at his sister with contorted features.

"The answer... you must read the answer."

"What was the question?" she mumbled.

"His real name," Nathaniel shouted, "I asked his name."

She listened as Gabriel wrestled Nathaniel away from the scene of destruction Eva had so despairingly organised. Nothing but the annihilation of Leviathan could save her brother from Bedlam. She murmured an apology over the sound of firing pistons. Letter by letter snapped into place as the angry fists of the mob crashed into the machine's hard exoskeleton. The message assembled itself for inspection. Eva was drawn towards the seductive answer, yet torn between her beliefs and love for her brother. Without looking, she moved away from Leviathan and recited two lines from the Bible.

"His heart is as firm as a stone; yea, as hard as a piece of the nether millstone. He beholdeth all high things. He is a king over all the children of pride."

The deserted chamber resounded to the hollow sounds of metal on metal as the dying mechanical curiosity was torn apart. The final answer presented itself without witness.

I AM WHO I AM

NOBODY WILL EVER LOVE YOU

"The World's a city full of crooked streets,
Death is the market place where all men meet,
If life was merchandise that men could buy,
the Rich could always live and the poor must die."

Epitaph in Stanwick, England. 1766

All staff killed on corporate business have the cost for a new body met by the group life policy. Too many deaths can result in a formal warning, and eventual suspension of your policy. Kate had never really considered the policy, until her DiamondStar smashed into the dock. For a minute she watched the rescue squad waddling towards her in their penguin-like protective suits, before the heat forced her eyes shut. As an optimist, Kate saw this as the first of her nine lives. Someone with a less positive outlook might have registered it as the start of her many deaths.

★

A circular column of water propelled the elevator-platform smoothly into the midnight sky. Jupiter dominated the vista with bands of swirling scarlet mutating just beyond perception. Jack stepped off the elevator to start his shift. Jack operated the new weather system that was parallel-intelligent, self-correcting, swift and efficient. Everything he was not.

After a handover with the early shift, he assessed the occluded front four miles to the west. The console buzzed with static and refused to respond. Too many power cables were crammed into its cluster of sockets. He jiggled a couple of wires and a spark flashed. He pulled the cable and everything went white. Jack's last thought was how he couldn't even kill himself without looking like an idiot.

★

Jack woke in a bleak aluminium room. A woman lay in a bed next to his.

"First death too?" she said. "There are vanilla clones in-vitrio for people without a policy that are classed as protected."

"You mean me?"

"I guess you couldn't afford a policy." She had meant to sound empathetic.

"I'm Jack," he said. "Or at least, I was."

"Good to meet you, Jack. I'm Kate, vee two."

★

The steam restricted his senses to the shower. Jack's unfamiliar body stood patiently, letting jets of hot water soothe him. Compared to his original frame, it was a definite improvement. He was taller, broader in the shoulders with near perfect skin. Despite all of this, he missed aspects of his old shape. The new fingers were too chubby. He felt clumsy and moved with the awkwardness common to a new ressie. The face was his major concern. The nose was

126

straight and the eyes clear blue, yet something disturbed him about the expression. It just wasn't him.

Reluctantly, he slid the shower door back. Like a butterfly, he emerged into the cold aluminium room and stretched his arms. Naked, he wandered to the corrugated wardrobe. He was still browsing the mediocre outfits when Kate startled him.

"How do you like it?" she gestured at his figure.

"Are these the best clothes?"

"The body's good, if you don't mind me saying."

"I'm not even sure what size I take."

Jack found a suit and fumbled with the buttons.

"Why was I protected? I feel like a whale," he said.

"Most people would be glad to still be alive."

"I'm not sure if I am."

"Glad, or alive?"

★

Kate wondered why she hadn't got herself killed before. Overall, she liked her new body. She remembered filling in the insurance form, ticking red hair, green eyes, olive skin, and a host of boxes about nose shape, ears, and lips. However, only certain combinations were available at gold membership. She could have red hair and brown eyes, or green eyes and blonde. Upgrades were expensive. The form seemed far more important now, and she realised some of her fashionable choices were not practical. She would try the body for a few months and engineer an accident if necessary.

"Check the small print," she said to herself in the elevator.

"Six months minimum," Jack said.

She turned her new green eyes on him.

"Sorry?"

"Before you can get a new body. It's a two-week replacement on platinum but that's a load more money."

"What makes…"

"Everybody does. Most people adapt in a month. Less, after a couple more deaths."

"How come you're such an expert suddenly?" Jack asked.

"I did some research. The nurse was driving me crazy with her sympathy."

The elevator-disc slowed its ascent, ready to deposit them back into life. Jack had decided he preferred being in limbo. Kate was ready to make some changes.

"Listen," she said. "Should we swap notes in a few days? One zombie to another?"

"I'd love to."

★

Kate was a different person at work and people commented. She was less demanding, a touch more thoughtful to her staff. The younger employees claimed she was in love. She was often seen with Jack; laughing in a jazz club, dancing on the beach, feeding each other sushi in Wai Ming's.

Six months later, Kate caught the quartermaster handling an illegal consignment. He pleaded, saying he needed the money to fund his own policy, since he was only a level 4B contractor. When that failed, he snatched a crowbar and beat her to death. It wasn't really murder, he reasoned. She would take a week to resurrect, time enough to leave the planet. Distance between the colonies meant law operated locally and rarely travelled well.

★

Kate had felt each blow as the quartermaster had poured out his anger. She had lost a nail first, then some teeth, and an eye. There had come a point when she had just hoped he would finish the job. The memory was still fresh, and she wondered if next time she should choose to have the death scene eliminated. She was very happy with body number three, though, and felt it was her best.

"Do you like it?"

Jack stared at the ceiling, the sheet draped diagonally across them.

"I love it. It's strange, but better."

"Better?"

"Shit, that doesn't sound good."

She slapped his chest.

"I mean exciting. Variety is the spice of life."

He wondered if that was why this relationship was working. There was always the thrill of the new. He couldn't say that. Instead he said, "I want you to pick my next body."

"You'd let me do that?"

"We could do it together. I don't want a giant nose."

"That's sweet."

"It's as important to you as me. And you've got better taste."

Kate mentally ran through a list she had already prepared. It was hard to see Jack any other way than his current shell, but there were a few tweaks she could make.

"Will you choose mine?" she asked.

"I'm not that crazy."

★

Jack went to see his father who lived in a pre-fab at the city's heart. There was nobody beyond thirty body-age at Jack's office, so it was a shock to see someone so old. His seventy-year-old father poured two brandies. They talked about mundane things to ease themselves into the harder conversations. Jack finally asked, "Have you given any more thought to planning for the future? Making

129

sure you're protected?" The word policy was to be avoided.

"I've been busy."

A silence fell between them. Jack looked at his father's left eye, which had turned golden-brown; as though it were rusting from inside. Tears streamed down his father's face unbidden and he dabbed at them every few minutes.

"How's the other one?" Jack gestured vaguely to the right.

"Not so good. I've got an appointment in two months."

"Why don't you go now? They can fix it."

"Who will look after your mother?"

"I could if you let me know the dates in advance."

"What if it goes wrong?"

His father topped up the drinks. Jack noticed his father was hunched from his old collarbone injury, and walked awkwardly. When he poured the brandy, he rested the bottle on the glass rim to make sure he didn't spill any.

"I'll be in hospital for a week if it goes well. If it goes wrong I'm blind."

They talked about Jack's mother. She was asleep in the bedroom. Jack would see her before he left, even though she no longer knew who he was.

They reminisced for a while and then his father leaned forward to impart a message, father to son.

"Last year, I decorated the bedroom. My knees aren't up to it anymore." Jack let him continue, not sure what response was expected. "I thought I was getting older. This year, I realised that was wrong. I'm not getting older. I'm a bloody old man, a bloody old man."

"Take the policy. Get a new body."

"What use is that when your mother can't? She doesn't need a new body."

"You could look after her for as long as it takes. If anything were to happen now, well…"

His father thought in silence.

"I'd have to go back to work," he said.

"There's plenty of work for people with your experience." That was a lie.

"We've done all we want to do," his father said.

It was a touch ironic that Jack was involved in a fatal accident on the way home. Although he was still counted as a valued employee, he vowed to fund his own policy and not leave his fate in the hands of the company.

★

The waiter twisted his mouth in distaste. It was considered a faux-pas to discuss your death in public. Kate was less and less concerned with other people's petty opinions. Since they had both died within a week, they sat opposite each other like strangers. Kate had suffered a massive heart attack. Her last body had been flawed.

"These things happen," she said. "At least the insurance company accepted responsibility and they've upgraded me to platinum."

The first course arrived. The usual fried insects.

"I've got a new urban myth," Kate said. "Apparently, the processing centre keep detailed stats, and top of the list is a woman. How many times do you think she's been resurrected?"

"It must be big or you wouldn't say it that way. Fifty? Sixty?"

"Two hundred and five."

"I thought it was only guaranteed to twenty?"

"No technical limit. Twenty is simply the insurance max before they hike the premiums."

The waiter topped up their blood-red drinks.

Jack lowered his voice.

"There's a man on Mars who can beat two hundred and five but you won't hear about him."

"Why not?"

"He's a government prisoner. They torture him to death, again and again."

"Why doesn't he talk?"

"It's a punishment, not an interrogation."

"What's he supposed to have done?" Kate asked.

"He was a terrorist. Planned some atrocity against ressies."

"That's almost funny. What was he going to do, kill us?" Kate looked around the restaurant at the perfectly toned bodies. "What have we become?"

★

For two years we survived. Jack was more surprised at the longevity of the relationship than our bodies. He was a different man to the one I had first met, in every sense. His deaths had been good for him, smoothing the edges. He switched jobs so he could afford his own policy. It gave him a feeling of confidence. You may think we're careless, but humanity is not a constant drive upwards in terms of life expectancy. The black plague hit the numbers hard, and during conquests the average life expectancy plummets. Frontier life is hard. Prior to the first planetary migrations, average life expectancy was approaching a hundred and ten. On Europa, it is closer to twenty-four. That's based on all resurrections being twenty at birth.

Two years without a death and then I had four in a row. Twice with radiation, one of which was my own fault, then poison (don't ask) and, most recently, environmental factors – aka company cock-up.

Jack was strange when I got back. I thought he didn't like the new body. We argued, and not the usual re-adjustment strains. I worried I had another faulty body. There were rumours of personalities switched and memories lost or changed.

Then Jack was killed. A group of teenagers in the old sector.

"They were messing about and it got out of hand," Jack explained. I think he was relieved to be dead, and refreshed.

We lay in bed.

"I'm sorry," he said. "For acting like a fool."

I felt guilty.

"I think," he said, "I was jealous of your new bodies. I was being left behind. You shone with each new resurrection."

"It was still me."

"This time you were different."

"This body is different."

"How?"

"I checked the fertility option."

★

It was harder to get pregnant than we realised. Sex is only a game when it has no deliberate aim other than pleasure. After that it becomes a business, and Jack and I approach our work in very different ways. The pregnancy was the longest time span I have ever experienced. During that time the embryo is massively vulnerable. It needs to implant, the placenta has to successfully kick-in, the cells need to multiply and grow without deformities. Which means I'm restricted. Suddenly my body is not my own. I can't play sports. There are foods I'm not allowed to eat. I have to be mindful of every action I take. The responsibility is crushing. I'm not growing a new body, those are relatively cheap. This is a new mind.

I worry about what our baby will look like. I have a recurring dream where I gave birth to a small crocodile with Jack's blue eyes. The eyes he had when I first met him.

My ovaries were loaded with my original genetics. It was a costly procedure. Jack had nothing to worry about. Sperm is automatically set-up for a man. I did wonder why that was standard and not optional. The downside was that our baby would be flawed physically, looking like a combination of our original shells. That can be changed easily enough when she is older.

We called her Ariadne. She is beautiful. And fragile. Now I dream she's made of glass and will shatter if I drop her. You can't get a policy until you're eight. The brain takes time to develop. Eight years is more than a lifetime. There are very few children in Europa.

★

We spend Sunday mornings at the beach. Even though Ariadne is fifteen months old I still have nightmares about her death. As I lie here trying to relax, I'm compelled to watch her. The waves are surf-quality, but crumble before they hit our stretch of beach. Jack once told me Europa was a wild animal and we should never assume she was tame. I watch the horizon and listen to the lapping waves as Europa breathes. Any slight change in the sound startles me. I imagine the water pulling into a tidal wave like a giant tongue to lick her wounds, sweeping Ariadne off the beach.

"How ya doin'."

I lie motionless. The vendor strolls past me. He begins haggling elsewhere and I watch Jack swing Ariadne over the waves. I scoop a handful of glass beads that form the sand, roll them against each other. Waste products from some project, converted into something passably useful. I sometimes wonder if they recycle our flesh.

I see a slender woman sprinting towards us. The chaos in her wake suggests trouble. A bulky man bars her path. Without breaking stride she swerves and places a two-fingered strike into his throat. I dive for Ariadne who is in the woman's direct path. Sweeping my daughter up, I turn my back to act as a shield. The woman hurtles past.

I never saw the stone the vendor threw. Missing its intended target, it caught me hard. I careered through the sand like an escape pod. Apparently, I clutched Ariadne tightly and after a few seconds of shock she bawled. My twitching body lay directly in front of Jack.

★

"There goes your no-claims bonus."

The man in a white gown smiled.

"Now you're platinum, you've been placed in the primary processing centre. It looks different, so don't be concerned if it doesn't seem familiar. You'll get a higher standard of service."

I was disorientated.

"Ariadne?"

"She's fine. So is Jack."

There was a sealed room in the primary centre filled with humming towers of black equipment. I asked an operative about them.

"That's the archive," he said. "Anyone who dies without a valid policy gets archived. If they have enough money they get a new body. Or somebody else can pay to have them resurrected. We used to keep them forever."

"Used to?"

"They take a lot of storage."

"How long then?"

"That depends on their role, contribution to society, that sort of stuff. There's a routine someone wrote to score everyone. It's a bit of a black art."

"How long?"

"Three or four weeks. Sometimes more if we need them for research."

★

I sat in the bedroom and sobbed. Jack was downstairs talking to Ariadne. *She didn't mean it,* he said. The truth was that she meant every word. Jack's voice was raised, he was losing his patience. Then Ariadne's voice pierced the bedroom door, stinging me again.

"Make her go," she said. "I want my mum."

I paid to have my policy permanently upgraded to platinum and three days later I stepped in front of an HG Transporter. The insurance company investigated, and despite the suspicious circumstances they upheld my claim. I returned with a body nearly identical to the previous one.

★

"We've only got ourselves to blame. Some technologies are too good to be held back, whatever the risks. Once the genie's out of the bottle..."

"We've turned ourselves into lab rats."

I went into the kitchen. Ariadne was squeezing brightly coloured sludge through her fingers.

"Mum, I know a great game we can play."

"What time does your father's cremation start?" I shouted back through the door to Jack.

"Two."

"I hate those places."

Jack came into the kitchen.

"They always put the crematorium in the worse part of town," I said.

"They put it where there's business."

"It seems a shame to have the cremation if we're going to bring him back."

"I don't want to bring him back." Jack was crying. I pretended not to see. "I mean, I do; but I won't."

"It's your choice."

"No, it was his."

★

I was shocked. Automatic rights to a policy had been rescinded. Officially, Europa was getting safer, but the death toll at my company continued to rise. I scanned the numbers to grasp the incongruity. The financial controller summed it up in one word. "Fashion," she said. "Curves, hazel eyes and cream skin are in this year."

The world is changing too fast. As a member of the management team, I'm still covered, and while that's a relief, it feels wrong.

★

Ariadne's eighth birthday party was a big celebration. After the children were in bed, we drank to annihilation, wilfully destroying brain cells and livers that would be replaced long before they failed.

I felt like I was in zero-g. My life was free of responsibility. This freedom came with a feeling of loss. A feeling that I was irrelevant. Ariadne had her own policy and was partially immortal. Alcohol loosened my tongue. I made a joke at Jack's expense, pointing out that his bodies seemed to get younger with each resurrection. Less body hair, less muscle, slimmer, as though he were ageing in reverse. Jack was upset. What hurt him most was that I was right.

★

Jack listened to Ariadne read one of his father's books. Kate came in from work.

"Discontinued. I can't believe it," she started, without a hello. "How can they discontinue teenage bodies?"

"There wasn't much demand. It doesn't make economic sense." Jack had already heard the news.

"So what happens when Ariadne dies?" Kate demanded.

Jack gestured for her to calm down. He left Ariadne and walked over to whisper, "They'll provide a vanilla clone, twenty-years old, and some false memories for the gaps."

"Gaps?"

"First period, first kiss, high-school prom, that sort of thing."

"You can't stick a ten-year mind in a twenty-year body," she hissed.

"She adapts faster than us."

"I wish I'd never left Earth."

"You don't mean that," he said, softly.

★

The woman with red hair reached the bar. A smartly dressed young man leaned at the counter. He swirled the ice in his glass and caught her eye.

"You again," she said.

"Ariadne."

"Nov or Pan?" she asked him.

"Sorry?"

"Novice – mental age less than body. Pan, two hundred years old and still seducing virgins."

"Is everything so black and white?" he said.

"Generally, yes. A vodka and cranberry," she added to the bar-girl.

"I know a great game we can play," the man said. Ariadne looked at him strangely. He continued.

"True or false. There was a woman who abandoned her policy

and then died in a freak accident. She never told her family she'd cancelled the policy. She left a note that said, *I have died so many times, why should I fear death?*"

"Dad?"

He smiled. "It's my latest body."

She looked it up and down slowly, "I like it."

He stood and took her arm gently.

"Nobody will ever love you," he said. "Nobody will ever love you like me."

They left the bar together.

GRIM

I will never see my daughter again. This is torture enough, but the worst part is the knowledge that this is my choice. For hours, I have sat in this cramped room and thought of nothing else. The walls are painted with guilt. The floorboards creak of betrayal. Every shadow hates me and they flicker as I pace the room, stalking like wolves. One shadow slides from the clock and creeps behind the bookcase. Another waits under the sofa with teeth bared. They should be scared of me, the father who rejects his child. I'm the monster.

I need to go out. I grab my jacket and open the front door. As I lock up, the phone screams. I count each of the twenty rings without moving, as though turned to stone. I know who's calling but I can't speak to them. The spell breaks once the ringing stops. I descend the long spiral stairway. Smacking the security door open I startle three teenagers sheltering in the entry tunnel and they scatter.

"Look into your heart," said my counsellor.

"What am I looking for?"

"Seeds."

"Spare me the bullshit."

"There must be something to nurture," she said.

"Who says I want to grow anything? I'm happy as I am."

"You're too active to wallow in misery for long."

"I've got a stubborn streak. I could wallow for years."

The sessions had been my wife's idea. There was a clearly defined process, like a series of signposts on a snaking path through hell. The first few weeks were about letting the anger out. I was amazed at how my soon-to-be-ex had managed to overlay her anger back across the years, what I thought were the good times. I had no idea things had been so bad. The formal process lasted twelve weeks by which point everyone agreed we were too far-gone; rescue was not an option.

The counsellor was called Rachel. Counselling is a monopoly as only women are allowed to be good at empathy. I seemed to hit it off with her, although counsellor/patient relationships were strictly taboo. Even so, I paid to see Rachel once a month, just as someone to talk with, even after the divorce came through. I told myself it was for my mental health. A week ago she asked me to do something she said I might think strange or childish. I was intrigued.

"I want you to read a story," she said. "Little Red Riding Hood."

"So we can talk about sexual predators?"

"Just read it. Don't think too much. Get the original text, not the kid's version."

That was a fortnight ago, but it feels like months. Parts of my life have been breaking off like icebergs, floating away to melt into nothing. Since my friends are all still married and I'm too old to mix with the singles crowd at work, I've taken to drifting myself.

I arrive at Lupo's. The jazz-funk music is pumping and there are a handful of people leaning against the bar. An aluminium alligator is silhouetted on the wall next to me, snapping at my bottle of Corona. I squeeze the lime down the narrow throat of the bottle and wipe sticky fingers on my jeans. I never thought I would be the sort of man to go to a bar alone. That's for losers and sleaze balls. I may be recently single, but I've still got a vestige of pride. I can't sit in my flat haunted by shadows and memories. *It's for the best*, I tell myself again. *We'll all get hurt more meeting one day a week, playing power games with my daughter as the weapon. One day, she'll understand, I hope.*

I pull the fairy tales out. I have a plain leather cover that hides the book so people don't think I'm weird. The stories are pretty familiar. It's only a couple of years since I was reading them to my daughter every night. We had a cosy routine, which she ruthlessly enforced as only children can. At bath time, her job was to choose the bubbles and empty too much luminous pink liquid into the water. There was plenty of wild splashing, often interrupted by demands to hide from pirates. A quick brush of hair followed the struggle to get pyjama's on, and the promise of a story was used as a bribe to finish her milk. Her favourite tales switched around, but some managed to retain their attraction. Normally the ones with monsters and violence.

In Lupo's, I look up from my book and watch two students. They're eating tapas, but from a distance it looks like a plate of sweets. They remind me of Hansel and Gretel, lost in a forest of bars. Pale and intellectual, they'd barely whet a witch's appetite. Working the tables at the far end of the bar is Rapunzel. She's the only waitress to wear her hair loose, with long brown locks that tumble down her back. She flicks her tresses whenever she sees a possible prince – or even a frog with potential. I always avoid sitting in her section. I'm not sure if I worry more about her flirting with me, or not flirting.

"Hello."

It's Rachel.

"Hey." I stand up. She seems to be on her own. There's a slight awkwardness as we've never met outside of her counselling office.

142

"Would you like a drink?" I ask.

"Sure, I'll have what you're having."

I expect an explanation for her presence in what I consider my bar. Etiquette suggests she should mention a meeting with some friends or her partner. Instead, she seems quite content to sit in silence and soak in the atmosphere. I'm pretty good at silence too, so I wait for her to make the conversation. She grins at me, wickedly, spotting the book with one glance. Her large eyes draw me in.

"So how's my big bad wolf?" she says.

"Is that a professional enquiry?"

"Only if you want me to charge you."

"I feel more like Jack."

"The giant killer?"

"And the beanstalk. I've sold the cow for some beans."

"And they're not magic?"

I take a swig from the Corona. Hansel and Gretel have been joined by Rumpelstiltskin. The place is slowly filling up. A Spanish waiter that could be a prince, were it not for his acne-scarred face, is lighting each candle. I'm not in the mood for any more deconstruction of my failing life. Rachel's drink arrives and we do some people-watching, swapping theories on the strangers around us. After a while, I decide it's my turn to ask the questions.

"So which fairy-tale character are you?"

"Guess."

I wonder if it's her training in psychology that enables her to turn the tables so easily, or if it's just that she's a woman.

"Little Red Riding Hood?" I say.

"That's your fantasy," she answers, "in fact, every man's fantasy." She deepens her voice, "Little Red Riding Hood was my first love. If I could have married her, it would have been perfect bliss." Then, in her normal tone, "Charles Dickens."

I tell her Charles Dickens was the first celebrity author and she's polite enough to pretend she hasn't heard that before. She stands up and reaches for my hand. "Come with me."

It feels alien to touch, breaking through a professional barrier constructed as carefully as the third little pig's house. Her hand is surprisingly cold. Outside, she releases my hand abruptly. We walk away from the town centre. The bars gradually give way to organic food shops, a specialist comic store, then kebab shops. We pass the turn for my flat and walk on another three blocks. I rarely venture in this direction. Perhaps I should leave a trail of shiny stones to find my way home in the moonlight.

We turn a corner and face the chequerboard front of the art-house cinema.

"My treat," she states and goes to buy tickets.

My last few trips to the cinema have been incredibly expensive, with babysitter fees accumulating, as I watch the latest disappointing blockbuster. This is different. The film is hot. There is a fragmented narrative with confusing timelines, sharp dialogue and raucous sex between twenty-something Italians. I am beginning to relax into the film when I feel Rachel's hand slide along my thigh.

Her apartment is less impressive than I expect for someone of her calibre. She gets me opening a bottle of red wine. Wrapping her arms around my waist from behind, she shifts one hand higher to squeeze my chest as I pour.

"Do you ever take anything?"

I'm not sure what she means.

"I've got something, if you'd like some fun," she says.

"Can I take it with alcohol?"

"Sure."

She disappears into the bathroom. I carry our drinks to place them on the wooden table by the sofa. I sit down, then stand up again, thinking I don't look good sitting that low. She emerges with a syringe in hand, giving it a tiny squirt. A spray of clear liquid fires out.

144

"Jesus, I thought it would be a pill, or something we could smoke."

"You're not scared of needles?"

"It seems a bit serious."

"This is the safest way. You'll just feel a small prick."

We laugh when we realise what she has said. She has my sleeve rolled up while we are still giggling.

"Say ow." The needle is in before I can speak. She dabs a piece of cotton wool on my arm and tells me to hold it in place. Putting the syringe down, she picks up her wine glass and looks at me. Her eyes hold a brilliance, spraying out passion like a diamond scatters light. She lingers over a sip of wine and swallows. Then she takes a second sip, never breaking eye contact. She leans towards me to reach around my neck with her free arm, pulling my head towards her face. Her scent is strong and not the typical floral or citrus perfumes, a lower tone from deep within the woods. She kisses me, releasing the wine. It explodes in my mouth.

We stagger into the bedroom and she pushes me on the bed. We tangle together like vines climbing a tower. She tears my shirt. I began to sit up and she shoves me flat.

"Slowly," she says, then adds: "I need candles."

She drifts away and I notice my chest is cut, a thin line of blood across one pectoral. It's tiny, like a paper cut. Rachel is circling the bed with candles. I'm amazed she has so many. There are some in old brass holders and others rammed into ancient looking bottles with beards of wax. There are even black candles, which I've never seen before. She turns off the light and pauses outside the circle. Slowly she peels off her clothes, revealing glimpses of skin as she glides in and out of candlelight.

"Talk to me," she whispers.

"Who's the wolf now?" I say.

"I am the moon," she almost sings the words.

"I am the sun," I make up as a reply, feeling stupid.

145

"And you burn for me."

The candles flare and I see her momentarily, standing with arms and legs spread wide, like a priest at an altar. I push myself up on my elbows then slump back down. My arms feel weak. The effort of lifting my head is a struggle but I manage to raise it just enough to see. The candles are pulsing. Her skin looks older and creased, her face haggard. Even her hair is coarser, cascading down in a torrent. Her breasts droop towards a black triangle of wiry hair. She looks like a witch. Her fingers are long and clawed. My head flops back on to the bed and lolls to one side. Only her eyes remain unchanged, those glittering eyes, burning and flashing like something from a fairy tale.

Waking Eye

When Predrag woke on his last day in paradise, he felt like a cigarette. That's not to say that he wanted to smoke, rather that he imagined himself to be a column of ash that might disintegrate if he moved too quickly. Rolling delicately out of bed, he toppled towards the bathroom. His mirror confirmed a nicotine-yellow complexion and red eyes. The long scar that disfigured his face was still unfamiliar and he traced its pattern with his finger. *It makes me look dangerous*, he thought. Today, he planned to abandon everything in exchange for hope.

"No regrets," he said, aloud.

Predrag was a stranger in this land. Everyone told him it was the finest place to live, paradise on Earth. They insisted that he should agree. The verdant city was set like an emerald in a ring of mountains. He admitted the vista was wonderful. It was the people he found shocking. His first impression had been of a city populated by tramps and this view had barely diminished. Also, the women were too thin, in his opinion, and the men obsessively developed muscles in order to push a mouse around a desk. It seemed as though the women might snap if the men embraced them, which explained why there were so few children.

"Nobody will care," he muttered.

His father had been a stranger in Predrag's hometown. He used to say that each successful foreigner makes a critical decision early in their displacement, to abandon their alien speech and attitudes. "It is necessary," he said, "so you can adopt the language and master the social etiquette. You must understand when it's acceptable to arrive late and what you should take as a gift to every type of event. By careful observation you can copy habits and gestures and learn the acceptable targets of ridicule. You may be able to masquerade as a local within a few years. By ten years, you'll feel you've succeeded, but it will be a generation before they accept you. During this process, you lose your original identity. Returning home is impossible, as it no longer exists outside of memory. *Exile is a wilderness,"* his father took pleasure in saying.

Predrag rejected this path, and much else his father taught him. He protected his differences so as to remain forever an outsider, which suited him very well. He liked it when people had to concentrate to understand his accent. He was naturally soft-spoken, which compelled them to listen even more carefully. He could act as he desired, within the boundaries of his stereotype. For most purposes, he was invisible. He liked to watch people in cafés, read obscure poets in his native tongue and eat the hearts of cinnamon buns. In this land of possibilities, Predrag conjured schemes to gain his fortune and daydreamed of returning in glory to his hometown.

At first, his thoughts had dwelt on the past. He recalled laughter, bleached grass and the smiles of girls he'd been too shy to talk to. Life in paradise was always purchased with a thousand small sacrifices. It was no great loss to surrender it today in return for hope.

"There is a pattern," he said. "I can feel it."

Pulling a canvas bag from under the bed, he selected a few items to squeeze inside. He took some T-shirts, a pair of jeans and some socks. Crushing them around the edge he formed a shape like a nest in the bag. He collected a box, which he placed delicately in the centre as though it might explode. Next to this, he placed some books. Covering everything up with three more shirts, he zipped the bag shut. He would never return to this room. Then, after saying a few words in prayer, he closed the door behind him, leaving the key in the lock.

Predrag reached the airport late, as planned. The woman at the check-in counter reminded him of Alicia. These days, so many women reminded him of Alicia, although their voices were tuneless in comparison. When Alicia spoke, her voice wavered; dropping a tone or shifting key like a sustained note in a saxophone solo. He had fallen in love with her voice first and then one by one, each imperfection. The lop-sided smile, the tilt of her head, and the ultra-white skin that gave her the appearance of a moonlit princess. Once upon a time, he had thought she was the person who would unlock this land and share its pleasures with him.

He sweated in the security line. It was a year since the last terrorist incident and he was relying on a return to apathy. He took off his shoes and belt. He emptied coins from his pocket and put them in a plastic tray while his bag went into the machine. A guard waved him through the metal gateway and glanced at his scar, but was busy chatting with a colleague. Every hope could end right here. His plan was based on human fallibility and a few simple tricks rather than the effectiveness of his precautions. The bag emerged from the black tunnel. He resisted the temptation to snatch it, sat down to tie his shoelaces and then walked away awkwardly, clutching the bag, trying to disguise his relief.

Predrag sat down in the window seat. The flight attendant chatted with two passengers, swapping 911 stories, as though they were badges of honour. He thought it would be much simpler if all loss could be given a gentle name and shared publicly.

As the plane soared, he took one last look backwards, before they banked away. It had been a long time since Predrag had admired the curved horizon from a plane's window. Today, the clouds were scattered like an armada. A thousand cumulus ships of war surrounding the city, anchored to their shadows.

Soon the new world below was comprised of irregular rectangles. The tiled earth reminded him of a child's puzzle where you had to shuffle the pieces to make a picture. He remembered that, in this type of game, there was always one piece missing.

Predrag ran his finger across the thin scar stretching from forehead to chin and thought of Alicia and the car accident. During weeks of recuperation, Predrag had stared at hospital walls until patterns emerged from the cracked paint. Months had passed without a word. Alicia wrote once – to say she found it too upsetting to see him.

The middle seat next to him was empty. Being six foot tall, Predrag was able to scan the rest of the cabin. Every seat was full, except for that one gap between him and the businessman in the aisle. Another missing piece, he thought. Another puzzle. He began to mentally shuffle the people around in the seats. He placed two attractive young things together and shifted the businessman back a row at a time to complete a line of six men in suits at the rear. No matter how much he shuffled the other passengers in his mind, there was no Alicia he could slide into the seat beside him.

She came to the hospital in the end, when he was nearly ready to leave. This was the last time he'd seen her. Alicia pulled a white sheet off a box the nurse had wheeled in. She studied Predrag for a reaction, as he stared at the aquarium. Moving his face closer to the tank, he saw something move, a thin strand like seaweed.

"You bought an optovic?"

"We say octopus, although I like your word more."

Predrag wondered if it was male or female. There were no obvious signs. *Maybe an octopus is like a worm*, he thought. He remembered learning at school that worms could breed on their own. They were both male and female at the same time, or perhaps they were neither. He forgot. He tapped the glass and a tentacle curled towards him, a flicker of white rippling along its arm like a smoke ring.

He named her Lullaby, because he liked the feel of the word rolling in his mouth, smooth as a pebble. Predrag lost Lullaby frequently. He would peer at the aquarium rocks, looking at every crevice. She could change colour to blend with the rocks. One afternoon, Lullaby vanished completely. For her, the ability to change colour was a comparatively simple task. Lullaby could change the very texture of her skin; smooth as a woman's thigh one moment, rough as stubble the next. It took Predrag nearly an hour to realise she'd slipped through his clumsy fingers, like so many other women.

"Lullaby's gone," he told the nurse.

"Don't be silly."

"She's left me."

The nurse pushed the door shut, and scanned the room nervously.

"If it's escaped the doctor will have us shot. You should have called her Murder."

Alicia had been a stranger in paradise too, possessing the same qualities as her gift. Capable of blending in anywhere, she was classless, with no hint of an accent. She never talked about her past, which made her impossible to track.

The nurse eventually found Lullaby, playing with a bottle of painkillers under the bed. When Predrag left hospital he made sure Lullaby was safe by using AstroTurf on the underside of the aquarium roof – a material he had read that an octopus hates to touch.

Alicia was not so easy to catch. There was no forwarding address at her flat. Friends and colleagues shrugged when Predrag quizzed them and stared at his scar while they talked. Few people had tried to make a connection with Alicia, as though they always knew she would move on as suddenly as she arrived. Predrag looked for a pattern, trying to resolve a mystery that he wasn't sure had a solution.

At the library near his flat, the young woman behind the counter treated Predrag like a fool on the assumption that anyone with a foreign accent must be stupid, uneducated or both. She said they had no call for self-help guides on predatory molluscs. The man at the pet warehouse was more helpful; he thought they ate shrimps.

"It will probably want them alive," he said, "but you could try them raw from the market."

"Yes."

"It won't live long," the man told him. "Two years at the most. They don't last."

"What does?" he answered.

A book from a second-hand store providing the missing piece of the puzzle, the fragile knowledge on which his dreams now rested.

The flight reached cruising altitude. Predrag squeezed past the businessman into the aisle. The flight attendants were busy further down the cabin. He opened the overhead locker and unzipped his bag. Peeling back the shirts, he found the box. Carefully unclipping the lock so as not to spill any of the water, he lifted the lid and checked Lullaby was safe. She was curled like a fossil, but a tentacle groped towards him. He knew better than to stroke her. He could be involved in a tug of war over his finger for another ten minutes. Shutting the lid, he collected his book and dropped the shirts back over the box, making sure it was adequately padded.

Again, he checked the picture showing the markings of the rare octopus he carried, found only along the coast of one island. This was his destination. He hoped the octopus was an elaborate invitation from Alicia.

He thought he was unlikely to be arrested smuggling an exotic animal into its country of origin, especially when he planned on releasing it. Lullaby and Predrag were both exiles. He'd decided it was time one of them should be set free.

CALIFORNIA DREAMING

Emily and I were going over the familiar patterns of our arguments when I received the signal. That meant this was a dream. Slowly, I took out a pistol and Emily fell silent. I raised the gun and pointed it directly at her head from a distance of some five feet. With a great deal of pleasure, I squeezed the trigger, expecting the dream to finish right there. In the enclosed space, the sound was deafening. I heard the neighbours rustling next door, woken from their apathy. *Now would be a good time for the dream to end*, I thought.

This all started three months ago in Las Brisas, a Mexican restaurant overlooking the beach at Laguna. I was with my sales team. Business talk soon flagged and we argued about whether one particularly stunning girl had plastic tits. The debate raged over burritos. We played spoof with beer caps and I lost. My forfeit was to discover the truth. Carnal knowledge was not required, although it would be a welcome bonus. I just needed the right angle to reveal the scars or some clever lines to encourage a confession.

"Good afternoon. I'm terribly sorry to disturb you." I tried my best to sound like Hugh Grant and let my English accent work its magic. We made introductions, and she told me her name was Tanya.

Tanya had perfectly symmetrical features and the requisite

blue-eyes and sand-gold hair for a CA surfer babe. In the blazing SoCal sun those features seemed a touch too pale, as though she was fading. I set myself the task of rescuing her. Not that she felt she needed this, but somehow I did. She worked in PR at Lucid TechSolutions of Paolo Alto, a classic Sand Hill Road-backed start-up. They offer products and services in Dream Management. The idea is to deliver control over your dreams, like your own virtual reality game.

"Have you ever had a lucid dream?" Tanya asked me.

"I'm not sure what you mean."

"Like when you're half-awake and dreaming, so you know this isn't real, and you can direct your dream. That's lucidity."

"Lucidity? Is that a real word?"

Americans love to give the English language lessons.

The first few workshops, Tanya had to drag me along. I only persevered because of the sex she held out as a bribe and delivered with vigour. My nights were certainly vivid, if not lucid. I bought a giant pair of goggles that monitored your eyes and could tell when you were in REM sleep. The device sent a chiming signal that I was conditioned to recognise so I could tell when I was dreaming.

The first time it worked I was having a nightmare set in the office, moving project files around. The folders were turning into snakes and getting bigger all the time. Then I heard the chime. I walked to the door and there was a post-it note in my handwriting that said *This is a dream*. I was suddenly aware that I could control my actions. What followed was like a cross between Beowulf and Halo. I grew swords from my fingertips and charged around chopping snakes into salami. It was incredible fun.

I was a convert. I began feigning tiredness so I could slip off to bed early. The first time I dreamt of Tanya it was spectacular. There was just one problem. Emily. We've been married nearly four years. People imagine she's easy-going. Underneath though, she bubbles with insecurities. It's like living on the slopes of a volcano. I guess she would say the same about me. We tried to resolve things and failed, leaving our issues to brood and grow.

Emily knew about the Lucid workshops. It was pretty hard to disguise the giant goggles in bed. I told her one of the guys at work had recommended it. The problems started when she woke me up.

"What were you dreaming?"

"I can't remember."

"Who's Tanya? You've moaned her name two nights in a row."

I bluffed through the conversation, but now I was paranoid. I'd never talked in my sleep before. I had to keep wearing the goggles and then if I saw Tanya I could walk away, reducing the chance of calling out her name again. Shortly after I told her about the problem, Tanya came round to the house during my waking hours. Luckily, Emily was out.

"You're rejecting me," Tanya said.

"Only in my dreams," I agreed.

"That's all that matters."

She picked up a plate and threw it at me. She was decent enough to conform to the stereotype of a crazed mistress and missed by several feet.

"Careful! We don't want Emily to find out," I said.

"Don't we?" She threw another plate.

"Jesus, you'll be boiling my rabbit next."

"No," she said, "I'm only half a cliché."

She crashed out of the house. I picked up the pieces. I had no idea those expensive Williams-Sonoma plates could shatter like that. I thought they were made of sterner stuff.

Initially, I thought I could keep the two women apart. Big mistake. With Tanya's increasing hysteria my world began to crack. Since I was scared of antagonising Tanya, I directed my anger at Emily. It was Tanya's suggestion that I confront Emily in my dreams. She thought subdued anger was damaging, and I would feel *empowered* once I gained *closure*. Her vocabulary, not mine.

That was easier said than done. It was years since I'd dreamt of Emily. You can't force yourself to dream of someone. Night after night, I tried counting Emilys in my sleep as though they were sheep. I herded her image into pens, and even visualised her leaping naked over rows of Ford Mustangs. Sometimes, I tried different cars when I got bored. She pranced and bounced over Ferrari's, Maserati, Range Rovers, and every type of SUV I could conjure up. Despite all of this, in my dreams I would only encounter old school friends, the surly gym receptionist and a hairdresser who used to rest my head on her breasts.

During the day, I was exhausted. Work became indistinct, a blurred activity that occurred between caffeine fixes. At home, I was tired and we argued more. We'd refined our skills so we could pick a fight over the smallest detail. The solid barriers dividing my life into neat boxes became veils of cobweb. I felt guilty about everything. The lack of time spent with Tanya, my betrayal of Emily, the failures at work. Reality became a sticky tangle of threads.

Standing here, looking at Emily slumped on the floor, I wonder if Lucid have a good attorney. I run through the mental checklist they taught me, to convince myself this is a dream. It's hard to concentrate with the sound of sirens approaching. One way of ending the dream for certain is to shoot myself. Apparently, that stuff about dying if you die in your sleep is a myth. Another alternative is to fight my way out, first-person shooter style, which might be fun while it lasts. Maybe I could steal a cop car like in GrandTheftAuto.

I listen as a siren arrives in a crescendo of wheels and brakes.

For the second time in a few minutes, I hear the distinctive chime that indicates a dream, and I notice it's coming from my pocket. I pull out my iPhone and the display flashes with Tanya's name. She borrowed my phone yesterday, or was that a dream? There are footsteps approaching the door. I feel the weight of the pistol in my hand. Placing the phone on the table, I walk upstairs, keeping the gun with me.

I walk into the master suite, then lie down on the bed. To the sound of our front door being smashed open, I close my eyes.

The Grass Oceans Beyond

I want to carve a heart in the tree, but my father's knife feels guilty in my hands. I breathe in deeply, but this high in the tree there's no air, only a green smell that can make you dizzy. I gaze across the canopy. The distance shifts in the summer heat, as though it's not real. It doesn't matter how high you climb, the horizon is never clear. I turn to the bark I've chosen as my page. Hearts are not easy. They need to be carved like two bass clefs with both sides matching. Mrs Luxton says cutting a tree makes it bleed. I don't think I love anyone enough to hurt a tree, although often I wish I did.

A movement disturbs the meadow. I swivel my head to see bobbing hair: two boys who must be tourists – grockles we call them. I sit very still and wish I hadn't worn my yellow dress. They jump the stile and run up the path crushed through the barley. At the crest, the taller boy turns and looks in my direction. He's bare-chested, with his shirt tied casually around his waist. He's a long way off and I don't think he saw me. They enter the copse that we call the island, because it's cast adrift amongst the crops. The boys are heading for the cave – like all the grockles do. I scramble down the tree as quickly as I can.

The best way to get to the other side fast is to reach the edge of the woods and run between the old trees that lean on the moss-covered walls. I duck under brambles and skip over rabbit holes and the abandoned badger sett that's crumbled the wall. My feet know the exact rhythm of steps and jumps on this secret path, so that it feels like I'm dancing. My favourite thing is that you stay hidden the whole time. When you're ready, you can cut deeper into the woods or rush into the sunshine flooding the field.

Following the moss-wall I leap down a tumbling drop where you have to hopscotch the rocks to avoid the mud that shelters here all summer. I reach the sweet-chestnut roots and squeeze through the shord, where there's a gap in both the hedge and wall. The back of the copse lies in front of me, a floating-island in the long-grass of the meadow. The crops are away to my right and even today, with no wind, the field sways gently and creaks like an old ship, as the barley cracks in the heat.

The grockles will already be on the winding path to the cave, unless the Rose brothers have ambushed them. Ian, Derek and Alan Rose. My mum says they're all doughnose and I should keep away.

I run through the meadow. Too much speed and the grass snatches your ankles until you fall over. I feel it whip my legs as my dress swishes behind me. The sun drips heat like treacle toffee, until everything is stuck together. I'm glad to finally slip beneath a camouflage of leaves and roll under the cool yew hedge. A branch grazes my arm and it stings. I don't make a sound.

I listen. Even the oodwail has stopped tapping. They must have reached the cave already. I'll need to be fast if I want to scare them. The cave is our place. Not for grockles with their crisp packets and wee. I leap from the earth bank to catch the branch and swing. You have to time this right or you fall into the gorse. I land softly on the sandy earth and shift into the ferns.

"Sshh! What was that?"

"It was the MONSTER!" The taller boy laughs. It sounds so good he shouts it again, "MONSTER!"

The smaller boy has blond curls and a T-Rex T-shirt. "Cut it out," he says.

They haven't brought a torch and they're nervous. Even bare-chest is reluctant to go further, but the younger boy expects it of him. I creep up the rocks at the side. They're not easy to climb. I crawl on my tummy and peep through the crack, careful not to block the light.

They should be talking in nervous squeaky voices by now and shouting *"hello"* to hear the echo. Instead, they're poking something with the stick. I can't see what it is. As they turn to come out of the cave, I jump down in front of the entrance to startle them. Bare-chest has brown skin, not the usual pink, red or white. He pulls one hand behind his back and I can see his eyes are wide-open and alert. T-Rex-shirt moves back a half-step behind his friend.

"What you got?" I demand.

"What's it to you?"

"This is my cave," I say and move forwards.

"Then these must be your eggs."

From behind his back bare-chest brings out his hand and gently opens his fist, hoping to get a reaction from me. I don't flinch. He holds two delicate pale-green eggs. One is cracked and inside I can see a slit-eye and scales.

I want it, even more than the bike that I nagged Dad about all summer. I want the brown-skinned boy to give it me.

"Vipers," the small kid says.

"Maybe something else." Bare-chest looks annoyed, like the other kid is talking down their dark-cave-find, in a forest where every rock is covered with witches' lichen.

"They're mine," I say.

The young kid seems scared, but Bare-chest is looking at me carefully. Derek Rose does that sometimes and I hate it. I don't mind it so much with this one.

"Finders keepers," he says, "although we might sell one."

"I ain't got any money," I tell him.

"There is one thing you could do." His eyes are alive and he

161

smiles. I like him and I want the egg. A green pine cone lands with a sudden phwump beside me. This time, I jump as much as T-Rex. Bare-chest grins. "The price of this egg is one kiss," he says.

I can see T-Rex is mad and he's going to say something. Before they can discuss it any more I nod yes. "Only one," I say firmly.

★

Summer has disintegrated. This year it only took a week. It wasn't the rain or the disappearance of the final grockles or even the fire-dance of leaves. Autumn strode in like a mean giant with the north-west wind and stole all the smiles. Proper job. Even the tractor man was distracted and silent as though he was lost. Those of a worse temper were to be avoided. The Rose brothers were cruel and dangerous enough in summer. I ran across them in the lower orchard, in a fall mood.

"Hey, look who it is. Your bint." That's Ian, the middle brother.

He looks at Derek who's chopping at something with his knife. Derek is my age and the youngest of the three. Derek starts most of the trouble. He always carries a knife as big as my father's and rumour says he used it once for real.

I turn to run back the way I've come.

Alan steps out from behind a tree. The eldest. He doesn't say much but he's the really nasty one. He finishes whatever trouble Derek starts. He's blocking my route. The Rose brothers are hard as a dog's head, thicker than blood, chaotic, callous, sick, vake, wild. That's what people say. The Rose brothers are to be avoided, that's what I think.

"You're just in time," Ian says.

"What for?" I ask.

"The Game."

The Game is a giant version of hide and seek with practically no boundaries. One team hunts and the other keeps moving.

There's no time limit, no specific goal, simply an endless pursuit. I think of my excuses, but don't offer them up. You need four to play. The sides are chosen without anything being said, since teams pair forever, like swans. I'm with Ian, the middle brother. At least I don't have to spend any time with Alan or Derek and his knife.

"Just the woods," Ian states the notional limits.

"Plus the island and the meadows," I say.

Alan nods and that's settled.

A coin is tossed and Ian calls tails for our team and wins. "We'll hide first," he says.

Alan starts counting slowly and quietly. Everything he does carries a threat. We have one hundred seconds to make our escape. Ian streaks away and all I can do is try to stay with him. He's the quickest runner on the estate and two years older than me. We have to get far enough away that the others can't see us. Without turning, I know that Derek will be cheating, secretly watching which way we go.

It doesn't take long for my lungs to start burning. Then my legs shake like jelly and my stomach hurts. There's something terrifying about being caught, even though it's a game.

We run across a field of tattered sheep and into the woods on the other side.

"Here," Ian says, but I can't see him. I look around and see the two brothers already tracing our path across the field.

"Where?" I say, in a hushed tone.

Ian's face pops out below a hedge and he holds back a branch. I slip into the ditch with him. He holds his finger to his mouth and makes a shush sound. We shuffle a little further along and crouch low. The ditch under the hedge forms a corridor, almost a room. The hawthorn is so thick you can't see in or out. I can hear the loud thump of my heart and the calls of Alan and Derek. They're combing the area, looking for any sign. Using their voices as weapons of intimidation, they try to flush us from shelter. They're coming closer.

"You're slow," Alan's voice, reprimanding his brother.

"They must be close." I hear the thwack as Derek hurls his knife into the ground in frustration, perhaps only ten yards away.

"They're probably miles away by now," Alan again.

Ian smiles at me and I want to laugh. I've stopped breathing in case they can hear. Now my stomach hurts from holding in the laughter. It's funny at first and then painful. Ian laughs silently too and we share the agony.

"I know something about her." Derek is trying to get some respect back from his big brother. I try and think what he might know, what he might say. My mind leaps to the cave and the summer. My guilt has been neatly folded and pushed deep in a drawer like my father's stolen knife. I suddenly recall the pine cone and see it hit the ground next to me. The stalk was cut clean through. Squirrels gnaw, knives cut.

The voices fade as they move past us. I strain to catch what Derek says next. I hear the rumble of his newly-broken voice but can't make out the words.

We give them five minutes and then crawl out. Ian leads us down the path. We talk quietly. Ian's not so bad when he's not with the others. Perhaps they're all better on their own. We stare out over the field. The island and its cave of secrets are a short distance ahead of us and up the hill. It's only a few hundred yards and the crop is high, but we would still be exposed if we crossed it.

"We'll have to use the path or we'll leave a track," Ian says.

I watch the waves moving across the surface of the field, gently breaking on the distant hedgerow. The path curves to the gate on one side of the peak where the tree line starts. It kinks three quarters of the way up and has two sharp switchbacks. I want to stay here and shelter under another hedge. Ian reads my mind.

"Once we're on the island, we can see them approach and

move off in the opposite direction. It makes us safe. The only risk is being seen as we cross the field, but they'll still be searching by Woodward's pond. Let's go."

I follow him and we move quickly along the path. We're about halfway up when they appear suddenly at the top of the hill, vaulting over the gate. They must have doubled back earlier. Derek moves off to one side of the path and Alan takes the other. They're walking slowly, cutting a trail through the faded barley. They have the advantage of the high ground. They'll be able to plummet down on us like falcons. We can never get past them running uphill. Ian says we need to split up as we sprint back to the woods and hope they only follow one of us.

"Go!" Ian shouts.

We hurtle down the path. Ian peels off to one side and heads for the stile in the far corner. I focus on the woods and once across the boundary I turn and rush along the edge. I swerve under brambles laden with green and red blackberries, then dance over the rabbit holes towards the shord. I hear Derek shouting and he sounds close. I've read enough fairy tales to know you should never look back.

Finally, the moss-wall tumbles over the slope's edge and I reach the familiar sweet-chestnut roots and throw myself through the gap. I count ten strides into the field and make three leaps sideways then fall to the ground. This is my secret place. The deep tractor rut through the meadow creates a dip where I can lie and be completely hidden. Even someone on the path or running below the ridge would miss me. I wait, counting heartbeats.

Less than ten fast beats and Derek appears at the wall. He steps into the shord and peers out towards the island. He stays forever, like a sailor seeking a ship on the horizon. He's thinking. I've never seen him do that before. Derek never stops cutting, twitching, throwing and stabbing. I don't want to know what he's thinking about. His face twists. He runs his tongue over his fat lips and all the time he stares towards the horizon. Just when I think I'll never breathe again, he vanishes. I lie there without moving for several minutes. Then I roll onto my back and watch the clouds, fierce and dark as warships, they gather and move inland. I use my summer memories to keep me warm.

When it gets too cold and the light starts failing I head home. Our lit houses huddle together in a small clearing. Coming out of the trees, I find the Rose brothers. Ian leans against the walnut tree. Derek sits idle on the swing and his elder brother props up the timber support.

"Well done. Where were you hiding?" asks Ian. I smile, but say nothing.

"They got me," he says.

"You cheated," Alan states and jabs his finger at me.

I know better than to argue with him. I shrug and wait for their judgement. I'm hoping my mum will call me for dinner first. They take a long time to decide what will happen next and they do it without speaking. I don't know which one will deliver the verdict. They stand motionless, apart from Derek pushing forwards and back on the swing, like they're communicating telepathically. Derek carves something in his kiffy way, but it's too dark to see what. He speaks first.

"There is one thing you could do," he says and smiles at this borrowed phrase. I bite my tongue. The others glance at him, not quite sure they've understood. "You could show us your snake egg." He carries on carving, but I know he's smirking.

I walk over to my house with all three hot like breath on my shoulder. I pull it out from under the shed, wrapped in a plastic bag. I give Derek the egg.

"You can keep it," I say.

"What's the price?" Derek asks.

"It's free."

"That's a shame," he says.

★

Winter comes early. The ground turns to rock. The pond gleams a thin and tempting invitation to play. I'm not fooled so easily anymore. I walk to the edge of the woods. The island has been unreachable for weeks, marooned by a sea of mud, earth toppling over in sodden crests. I decide to visit the cave.

I have gloves where my fingertips poke out. I wriggle my fingers and begin to cross the frozen earth to the island. It's slippery and parts give way, collapsing beneath my feet like weak breakers on the board-sands. I'm really cold by the time I get there. It's silent and the air seems to fix sounds as though they were needled in place by icicles. The trees are stripped bare apart from the evergreens by the cave. The ground crunches underfoot. I stare into the cave, then sense someone watching me.

"Look who it is," Derek says.

I'm cornered with the cave behind me. I look for his brothers, but for once he's alone.

"You look pretty," he says.

I start to move sideways but Derek steps across. He's ulking. "You like snakes, don't you?" he says, in a voice like his eldest brother, quiet and full of intent.

"Yes," I answer.

"I'm going to show you one."

He points over my shoulder to the gawping mouth of the cave. "In there."

For each pace forward he takes, I make one back. As I move into the cave, the outside world retreats into a ring of white frost with Derek silhouetted. For once, he has something other than a knife in his hand. Its red-head pokes out of his trousers and he points it at me, moving his hand slowly, like he was stroking a pet. "Hiss," he murmurs, and the sound echoes inside the cave.

I wasn't going to come to the island today. I was going to climb a tree and carve a heart. That's why I have my father's knife. I stand still as Derek moves towards me. The knife no longer feels guilty.

"Let me see it," I say.

I guess the heart will have to wait.

The blade catches a spark of pale light. Derek crumples and I run past him. I still don't know if trees bleed, but snakes do.

My legs propel me out of the copse with my breath billowing like clouds of sea fog. I veer away from home, and know I'm on a different course now. I steer away from the island towards the grass oceans beyond.

ACKNOWLEDGEMENTS

'The Cobblestones Sparkle' published in *Bristol Short Story Prize Anthology,* 2008.

'Breeding Monsters' published in *Words with Jam* magazine, and the associated anthology, *An Earthless Melting Pot,* 2013.

'Driftwood' published in *Scrawl,* 2006.

'Beetles & Butterflies' prize winning story from *Wells Festival of Literature,* 2006.

'Appetite' published in *The Pestle,* 2006.

'14 Cannibal Kings' published by *BrightonCOW,* 2011.

16 Military Wives
Words and Music by Colin Meloy
Copyright (c) 2008 Music Of Stage Three and Osterozhna! Music
All Rights Administered by BMG Rights Management (US) LLC
All Rights Reserved Used by Permission
Reprinted by Permission of Hal Leonard Corporation

'White Mice' published in *Salt Horizon Review*, 2008.

'Killer' published in *The Big Issue in the North Award for Short Fiction anthology*, 2013.

'I Wish I Was Like You' first published in *The London Magazine*, 2008.
'Bewildered' first published in the *Jericho* anthology by Cinnamon Press, 2012.

'Something To Remember Me By' winner of the H E Bates short story prize, 2012.

'Sibling Games' published in *Momaya Review*, 2010.

'When All The World Shines' published in *The London Magazine*, 2009.

'A Question Of Madness' published in the *Dogstar* anthology by Leaf books, 2007.

'Nobody Will Ever Love You' published in *Succour*, 2007.

'Grim' published in *Invisible Ink*, 2007 as 'Monsters & Violence'

'Waking Eye' published in *Brand*, 2011.

'California Dreaming' published by *InkTears*, 2010.

'The Grass Oceans Beyond' published in *Riptide*, 2012.

A NOTE FROM THE AUTHOR

Many of these stories were written on planes flying from place to place in America and across the Atlantic, while working at a company based out of Southern California called DATAllegro. The people I worked with inspired, reviewed and in some cases actively participated in the development of these stories. I would thank everyone involved in DATAllegro (which was great fun!), and highlight Stuart Frost, Julie Frost, Mark Thacker, Dave Salch, Cliff Currie, Patrick Lilley, Jesse Fountain, Andy Mouacdie, Ian Giles and Umair Waheed in particular for their support in making these stories happen. Part of the reason I spent so much time on aircraft was that I was finishing a Creative Writing qualification at Oxford University while living in the USA, a minor complication! There were fantastic people on my course, talented writers, and I learnt many things from every one of them. Thank you. My course tutor was the marvellous Stephanie Hale, who continues to be an inspiration to myself and many other writers, and I would also thank Clare Morgan who challenged and pushed me in the second year. I must also thank Sally Bayley from Oxford University, a wonderful writer, editor, teacher and friend.

I've borrowed some names from real-life to use in these stories, but if you spot your name that doesn't mean the character is you, it just means that I like your name! However, there are some people

NOBODY WILL EVER LOVE YOU

that appear in these stories as genuine representations of themselves, although in those cases the names are usually disguised. They know who they are, but I'd like to call out Alan and Anne for appearing in *Sibling Games,* Simon Pinnock for featuring in many prize-winning stories based on our teenage adventures, Ian Homer who will recognise the game in *The Grass Oceans Beyond* and was both the fastest sprinter and the best carver of balsa wood planes ever, Nasir Khan for his cameo in *Bewildered*, and Mark Hounslow who is standing just offstage in several stories and was wise enough to check the facts in *Killer* to make sure I really wasn't a serial murderer.

My work has been improved by clear-eyed editing in various journals, but more importantly my passion and enthusiasm for writing has been fuelled by the positive encouragement provided by every editor or judge that picked my story and deemed it worthy of attention. I thank all of you, and would emphasize Anthony Banks for publishing *Nobody Will Ever Love You* in *Succour*, Sara-Mae Tuson for spotting that story and subsequently publishing my work in both the London Magazine and Trespass, and for her collaboration on InkTears, which has been invaluable. I have to thank David Gaffney both for his role as a judge in the Big Issue in the North competition that selected my story as the winner, but perhaps more importantly for making me laugh at many literary events and revealing the joy of flash fiction. I want to thank Katie Fforde and Jill Patton Walsh for choosing my stories in competitions and giving me feedback that made me feel like a *real* writer.

Finally, I must thank my extended family; Helen for her tremendous work in growing InkTears, Mike for reading just about everything I've written and providing constructive and valuable criticism, and Scott for providing a different perspective. I promise to write about bayonets another time Scott!

A NOTE FROM THE AUTHOR

★

Of course, this book would never have happened without my immediate family, Gillian & Freya, who gave me time to write and edit, despite many other pressures on our lives, and were the inspiration behind so many stories. Thank you.